THE GREAT HEXPECTATIONS NOVELLA BOOK ONE

Possessed

AWARD WINNING AUTHOR

MARIE F CROW

AUTHOR OF THE RISEN SERIES

Copyright

Possessed is a work of fiction. All names, characters, locations, and incidents are the products of the author's imagination or are used fictitiously. Any resemblance to actual events, locales, or persons, living or dead, is entirely coincidental.

Editing by KP Editing
Cover Design & Formatting by KP Designs
- www.kpdesignshop.com
Published by Kingston Publishing Company
- www.kingstonpublishing.com

Table of Contents

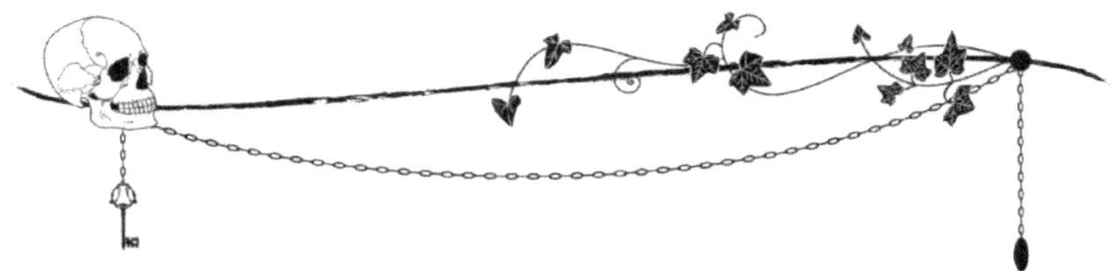

He doesn't just want to claim my body. He wants to pierce the depths of my desires until my soul itself is bound to him, marked forever as his. I will be possessed endlessly. And it's not by the man I once thought would hold me.

THE GREAT HEXPECTATIONS NOVELLA BOOK ONE

Possessed

Hell hasn't forgotten Harper—and neither has its ruler. They've been watching, waiting. And this time, not even Jedrek may be able to save her.

Harper's gift of summoning the dead has gone unchecked, so long as the souls she called forth were returned. Heaven turned a blind eye. Hell made an unspoken truce. But now, the spirits she has been summoning are returning broken and fragmented... and hell is furious. They want their debt paid.

Jedrek, torn between duty to his master and the love he swore he'd never feel, is given a choice. He must collect what's owed or uncover why Harper is being haunted by the very souls she was meant to release. To find the truth, Jedrek must delve into Harper's darkness the only way he knows how...by tasting it for himself.

And if he's too late? They both burn.

Content Warning: *This book is a work of fiction intended for mature audiences (18+). It contains explicit sexual content, strong language, and violent encounters that may be disturbing for some readers.*
The book boyfriends within these pages don't play well with strangers… though sometimes they do play with each other. Proceed with caution, curiosity, and maybe a fan nearby. Reader discretion is advised.

The overhead streetlights beat down like torture, strobing relentlessly in their pattern. The night has been a complete failure. The family who hired me to call back dear ol' Aunty forgot to mention she'd been cremated. They didn't seem to understand that no body *in* the grave means no body *above* the grave either. Luckily, their uncle had the same information they needed, and I doubled my fee thanks to their stupidity.

Jedrek's constant humming along with whatever song is on the radio is setting my brain on fire. His relentless flirting with the youngest woman attending tonight was beyond predictable. How someone of his age can still need that much adoration speaks of the male ego loud enough to drown any good mood I might have salvaged from my raw nerves. Knowing the demon is practically indestructible, I can't help but wonder if stabbing him a few dozen times would make me feel better.

"It could have gone worse," he finally says, knowing me better than I'd like to admit.

My red curls float in the air conditioning of the car tickling my neck when I turn to stare at him with a look of complete disregard.

"Is that your final thoughts on the matter?" I ask flatly. "Because I really don't want hear it."

Jedrek nods, keeping his face forward to watch the road. "Not in a talking mood, I see. Here I was so eager to discuss your recent life choices."

"Oh, I bet you were." I mutter, returning to rest my head against the glass. "We could always discuss your choices tonight."

I feel his movement to look at me, watching the reflection of him smile at me amid the blurred scenery passing by us.

"There are no rules to how I make the deals, Harper," he says with pride, as though tonight's conquests were trophies. "Or what I promise to achieve them."

"Do they even know where your promises will lead them?" I ask, only half caring, knowing I should care more, but I just don't have it in me.

Jedrek shrugs without a care. "Where their minds were when agreeing isn't really my problem."

"Disgusting," I whisper to the window.

"You disturb the dead for money, Harper," he reminds me. "Not sure if you can really stand on a pedestal of morals."

I'm elated when his car pulls in front of the house. It seems to have become more of a hostel than haven as of late. Morality is not a debate I want to have with this man. Especially not when my human fibers are so thin with everything being asked of me by those I'm constantly being asked to save.

The black classic car door is heavy to open. Maybe it has its own ghosts that are attempting to caution my climbing temper as a match against his unforgiving wit. It's even harder to close when I climb from the leather interior. Jedrek is watching me from his side, resting his upper body on the roof of the car far from my crumbling mental state, but those blue eyes of his are shining with pure amusement over my frustrations.

"It's a door," he tells me, still resting on his car. "Try pushing it."

"You're pushing it," I tell him, finally slamming it.

"Good girl," he winks. "I knew you could do it."

"I hate you," I toss over my shoulder as I head into the house.

His laughter trails behind me mocking my hope once he dropped me off he would be happy to find another target to annoy for the night.

"I don't really believe that," he whispers into my ear as I fumble with the door's lock.

Pushing him from me, I open the door with a sound of disgust. "That's because you think everything with a vagina just has to have you."

"Not just a vagina," he adds with an off-handed beat. "My side doesn't judge, remember?"

The house reeks of Regan's incense. It tends to hang in the air, floating around without a reference of time or a need for one. Much like our new housemate, it has taken over almost every living space without a care to whom it may bother with its presence.

I shuffle through the pile of mail doing my best to ignore him with hopes he'll grow bored. "Doesn't judge. Doesn't have rules. Loose on morals. Got it. Sounds like a real winner of a pamphlet insert."

He toys with the ringlets tightly coiled around my face. "Might be why we get inserted more."

Normally, that might have gotten a smile from me. A small smirk at very least, but not tonight. Tonight, it turns my stomach as I remember him doing something very similar with the women from tonight to win them to his cause. Their souls will be his now, added to the constant battle, and game, between Heaven and Hell for control through pure numbers.

"How can you be proud of yourself?" I ask him. "Those women think they are getting a date. A fucking date. They have no idea what you are, or what they have done, or anything about what you are almost bragging about."

"What mortals know or don't know is not my problem, Harper," he tells the skin of my neck. "Besides, it's not as if we hand out business cards announcing ourselves. If mortals really knew what walks around them every day, we'd have to slaughter them."

"So, that's how you accept what you're doing? Make it not bother you? You tell yourself you're really saving them?" I mockingly ask him.

His soft laugh sends shivers in places I refuse to admit. "Who said it bothers me?"

"Get the fuck off me!" I shove him, not caring I'm unable to move him unless he wants to be moved. I just want him to know I want him away from me and somehow that makes complete sense in the ramblings of my bitterness.

"You're acting like a bitch," Jedrek dares to tell me in my current mood.

The last sliver of sanity I still hold in the front of my brain watches him drop his body to the couch I hate for reasons which seem to grow each time I encounter it. The rest of my brain is a dumpster fire of encouragement to let the world burn down around me starting with the smart-ass demon before me.

"Call me a bitch again and see what happens," I warn him, knowing fully well he's going to call me a bitch, again. He won't be able to help himself. It's Jedrek.

His passive lips curve into the deadly smirk which has carved his trail through history upon hearing my dare, slowly, pulling the one syllable word into something longer somehow. "Bitch," he whispers to me.

Framed by his black hair, his eyes appear to brighten, almost glowing with mischief as our eyes lock waiting for my response. Lounging, completely relaxed, his black shirt clings to him like a second skin. It ripples and ridges as it flows into the dark jeans. Jedrek has always known how to wear this body to benefit his every mood and need. This moment is no different and he's not bothering to hide his enjoyment of my traveling eyes.

"Now you're acting like a bitch in heat," he comments. "Think we've found your problem."

"I don't have a problem," I snap, annoyed with myself for falling so easily for his ego-feeding games. "If I do, it's you."

The red curls are suddenly heavy from summer's unrelenting humidity. Even at night, the air seems to be weighted, pulling the world closer around me than I enjoy it. When my job is to summon the dead, there are certain smells I don't want that close to me. Their families wailing in the background is often nerve grating enough, but having to keep a pleasant smile while the one I have been paid to bring back for whatever reason sucks the blood from my arm in the summer months is antagonizing to the senses. Jedrek insisting to attend my jobs every night out-of-the-blue only adds to the antagonism to my senses.

Jedrek tilts his head back-and-forth mocking me. "So, you have a problem, or you don't have a problem? Help me keep up."

"I don't have a problem," I tell him through gritted teeth, slamming my purse down on the coffee table along with the large knife I used tonight, the empty water bottle, my phone and something else I had in my jean's pocket for extra noise and satisfaction of slamming something down.

He watches my mini fit without expression. "Clearly."

"I don't have a problem," I repeat again, pausing between each word as frustration eats further away at my sanity.

He smiles at me, nodding slowly, mocking wide eyes while remaining silent.

"Why are you here?" I ask, defeated by the conversation, feeling my whole body sag from the stress trying to drown me.

Jedrick stares at me, his body becoming motionless, triggering my predator response to his stalking eyes. He's dropped the human pretense he carries around like an actor on a constant stage. His chest no longer rises and falls with a need for air. There is no absent-minded fidgeting or random moving of limbs for comfort to appear human. There is just his soul-searing blue eyes locked with mine, somehow pulling my heart rate to an impossible speed.

A normal person would feel the need to run under such a gaze. Their brain would tell them something is dangerous in the room, to get out, to save themselves. Mine is tightening, clenching, something low and hungry inside of me. My breath catches under the gaze. I'm already mentally feeling his torturous mouth on my body before I can stop myself.

"Stop that," I whisper.

"I'm not doing anything, Harper," he whispers back. "I haven't even moved."

Closing my eyes, I almost sway with the need to have the scent of his skin wrapped around me. "You know exactly what the fuck you are doing."

"Tell me again how you don't have a problem," he whispers from somewhere closer in the room.

Run. Flee. Save yourself. It's all I can think about. If he touches me, I will break. I will crumble before him. No one can tear my soul apart like he can with such a simple action or the softest of words. The basement stairs to my room look like welcoming arms to safety. If I can reach them before he can reach me, I might just survive this encounter.

His voice follows me upon my retreat. "Run if you want. I'll just follow, Harper. You might hate me, but you need me. And I don't mind the scent of a scared witch in the air."

The stairs come rushing at me as if gravity is cheering for my downfall or my admirable klutz gene is once again choosing the best time to arrive. Either way, I have to almost skip down the last few to recover from my panic and, more importantly, my ankles. Mostly my ankles. My panic, however, stays lodged in my throat, squeezing my heart in a painful rhythm knowing he's somewhere behind me. I just pulled the classic horror movie bimbo move running to hide in the room without an exit. My pride won't let me try to squeeze through the window to only be caught with my ass high in the air because I couldn't fit it through in time. I'm officially screwed.

"Harper," he calls from the top of the stairs, soft and sing-song.

I know what he wants. My body knows exactly what he wants and it is betraying me answering his call with its own soft cry from my throat despite my best effort to silence it. The memory of his touch, his taste, his scent is always present in my mind when he is around me. It's carved into me. Demons and witches aren't supposed to share this bond, but just the sound of his voice when he lowers it can make my throat catch with a need I hadn't known existed until him. And he's right, I hate him for it.

I hate that I want him despite my better judgement, which most days is barely better than a bored toddler's. I hate that he knows that I want him. I hate most of all that *everyone* knows it. I'm the defender of a Coven, a necromancer feared by many. Not this coward, hiding from a demon whose idea of foreplay is tying knots out of my clit with his tongue before having mind melting sex. Yet, here I am, slowly walking backwards as his shadow moves down the stairs towards me.

"Harper," he calls, voice lilting, "I can smell you."

"I showered," I hoarsely whisper to him. "It's new lotion."

"I can smell that, too," he matches my whisper like a true predator. "But that's not what I am enjoying."

I'm still trying to walk backwards from him until there's nowhere left when he rounds the corner of the stairs to stand in front of me. "Oh?" I managed, voice brittle. "Well, that's awkward."

Jedrek tilts his head, smiling a smile that lights his eyes. "You've run out of room my littlest witch. Wherever will you go now?"

"Don't suppose you'll step aside and let me slip by?" I ask, breathless.

The charming smile he was just wearing melts to something playfully sinister. His light blue eyes darken quickly as if storm clouds have rolled over a sun-filled afternoon. A shiver of anticipation rolls over my body causing my lips to part further when the gasp slips from them.

"Every time you play this little game," he says, low and velvet. "you pretend to resist. I gladly chase you. You play coy when cornered. I gladly, eagerly, initiate. You cave without complaint the moment I kiss you. Then you will fearlessly fuck me anyway I want you, any position I want you. We could save so much time, Harper, without your little game."

"Was there a question in there?" I ask, watching him inch forward with his eyes never leaving mine.

His smile turns deadly. I've seen this smile before. He loves to flash it right before he tears into someone he no longer has the patience to leave living. Here it is upon those soft pink lips taunting me.

"Why would I do that?" he asks, lifting one eyebrow with his question. "You once told me it's considered bad manners to play with my food before eating it."

I can feel my knees buckle momentarily upon hearing his response before I can compose myself.

His fingertips skim my cheek, his eyes watching the path they are gently taking along my skin. "And I plan to eat everything you offer me tonight."

"What are you in the mood for?" I ask, desperately trying for any last seconds of self-preservation. "Pizza? Chinese?"

Jedrick's eyes dart from his fingertips to my eyes. "Why do you play coy?" he asks me. "I know exactly what those eyes are begging me to do to you. All you have to do is ask, Harper. All you've ever had to do is ask."

My tongue sticks to the roof of my mouth.

His pale skin, dark hair, and those blue eyes pin me in place. His pale pink lips so often formed amid jokes at my expense hang slack, frozen in a neutral position while he watches me, waiting to see what I'm going to do with his body so close to mine. Honestly, so am I.

"I'm not sure what I'm begging for," I whisper, though knowing that I want to feel his hands on me again.

I want to feel the weight of his body upon me, pressing me down onto the bed. The warmth of his mouth trailing along places I still blush when caught fantasying about him tasting. The depths of me are tightening, almost hurting, with a need to feel him pushing himself inside of me, stretching me, forcing my body to accept his length and width without mercy despite its protests. How do you ask for something such as that?

"Release," he whispers. "How many jobs have you taken recently, Harper? How many voices are floating around in that head of yours when you can't sleep? How many shadows are stalking you from the dark corners of the rooms you are in?"

"Is this rhetorical?" I ask, watching his fingers hover dangerously close with fear over where they may explore next.

He ignores me completely. "I can feel them clinging to you, whispering amid your own mental demons you've collected along the way. I can taste their desperation to reach through those walls of yours, wearing you thin. Let me give you release from them. Let me take the fragments of the dead from you, as only I can, Harper. Let me fuck you."

The women tonight would have already crawled onto the bed, parted her legs for him or at the very least asked in which position would he like them. Here I am standing frozen before him like some sacrificial virgin afraid of the big, bad wolf in front of me even though he's devoured me plenty of times before now.

"I can handle it," I tell him, knowing it's a lie. "I don't need your help." I know that's also a lie. "Nor do I want it." Still, a lie. If I keep practicing, I might even convince myself, maybe not him, but maybe myself.

Cupping my chin, my face is locked in a vice of his strength, lifting me to where I am an even height to his. Dropping his head to run his nose the length of my neck, behind my ear, I feel him whisper against that sensitive skin, "That's not what your scent is telling me, littlest witch."

"Ever have a feeling you've had a conversation before?" I meekly whisper back to him.

His soft laughter of amusement causes my skin to beg for him. "Every damn time I'm around you."

"Why have you really been following me around?" I ask, feeling slightly braver with his face tucked away from mine. "No word games. No jokes. No grey area of the two. What is really happening here?"

Jedrek doesn't answer me. Instead, he continues to tenderly play with the side of my neck. I know this routine. He's carefully choosing his words, trying to decide how much he can tell me without breaking some promise he's given another. The only person who truly holds Jedrek's leash is his master. Yes. That master. Lucifer himself.

I sigh, wondering how I am supposed to keep the Coven safe when I'm always piecing things together too late?

"You didn't really think I believed you came all way up here to spend a night with me just because you had an itch, did you?" I press with my self-depreciation on display. "Or that I believe you have been so overcome with concern for me lately that you've just had to go on every job with me as of late? Please don't insult me. I have enough people doing that in my life already."

"You're half right," Jedrek admits, trailing his hand down in defeat when hearing my request. "Not that I would ever *not* travel all the way here to spend a night with you, should either of us have an itch," he begins as his walk of defeat takes him away from me, simmering the lust and his ego. "Don't ever second guess your ability to stir my desires, Harper. Or my desire to stir your desires if you need me."

Tilting my head, I can feel my smirk I use like armor already upon my face. "But…?" I leave it open, letting him drop the blade I'm sure will cut me to the bone.

Pausing, he glances over his shoulder nearest to me. "There is no 'but' on that, my littlest witch. I crave you the way I crave their pleading screams right before they realize what they have agreed to do. I want you to need me the same way I need them. I want my name on your tongue, tearing from your throat, etched on my skin from your nails. I want to be the one you call on when scared, to protect you, from not only your enemies, but also yourself. There is no 'but', Harper. You just won't allow it to be."

"You want more than I'm willing to give," I shrug, refusing to be swayed by those broken little boy blue eyes he shows only me.

He toys with a forgotten bra on my bed with the curiosity of a teen. "Just everything," he mutters, as he traces the lace pattern with his fingers. "I only want everything."

"Enough," I sigh again taking the discarded clothing from him seeing we are back to his games. "Why are you really here, Jedrek?"

Sitting a little too casually on my bed for my inner protective walls to be comfortable with, I finally get the answer he's been trying to avoid giving me with his games, flirting and dangerous promises.

"They are coming for you, Harper. It's better you let me fuck you than let them fuck with you, but…," he says pulling that word out to mock me, "I suppose it's up to you. Isn't it, littlest witch?"

3

Once upon a time, the floor would have shifted beneath me at hearing such a headline from him. Now? No. Now it's just another day on an endless calendar. The seasons may change, but the climate always stays the same.

Crossing my arms like a barrier between us, I dare to stand in front of him. "Someone is always coming for me." His eyes light up, with some remark, but my glare steals it from him. "It's never sent you to this length of dramatics."

Falling back onto the bed, his eyes stay locked onto me the entire time. "I tell you you're in danger, and you rush off to confront it like someone demanding to speak with a manager. I thought I'd try something different this time. Something maybe a little more fun for both of us. Now, climb up here, and let's play a little game of 'what has Harper been up to'?"

"Do you ever stop?" I ask, rolling my eyes at his eagerness.

"Not unless you beg." Jedrek smirks, pretending to be afraid of the outcome of his joke. He even laughs before motioning for me with his extended hands, inviting me to come join him on the bed like a playful white flag.

Why am I allowing him to pull me on top of him? That is the question I should be asking myself. Instead, I'm wondering why *he* is feeling the need for me to be close to him. Why is he so damn eager to help me? Or is it his release he's really chasing?

His hands slip beneath my shirt, tracing random patterns on my stomach. "You need to let me fuck you."

The way his eyes are locked on me as he says it makes my thighs tighten around him. "I'm not really in the mood," I gasp, feeling his hands growing braver.

"I can fix that," Jedrek promises.

I don't fight the moan that slips from my throat. For most couples, such a promise would means sweet, gentle pleasure before giving into the passion of their bodies. When you swim in the pools of Hell, heat has a different meaning and he's shown me pools I never would have dreamed could be filled with such delights.

The obsidian blade he produces from behind his back might as well have crawled into the depths of my chest to drag the whimper from me.

"There's those hungry green eyes of yours," he coaxes. "Who is going first, my hungry girl?"

I drop to my hands, hovering above him, letting my red curls fall around us like a curtain ready to be drawn back for the start of our show. "You," I barely manage to tell him with my excitement.

"You are the sweetest thing," he murmurs against my mouth, handing me the blade without a hesitation.

There's no need to bind him. He won't resist what I am about to do to him. After all, he's the one who taught me it, the one who begs me to do it with him and the one who answers my desires for it - bloodletting. For me, it's the dark secret of shared obsession and control I can only indulge with him. A moment of safety in the darkest corner of my mind. For him, it's the simple need to enjoy pain and taste the taste of me in ways only he is allowed. It's a secret Roman, my other lover, will never know. A secret that makes Jedrek smirk when Roman tries to boast about our relationship in front of him.

If he removed his shirt, or if I did, I can't seem to remember. I know it's my hands fighting with the belt of his jeans until he takes over. I never had patience for a man who needs me to undress him. There are better uses of my time. Like how we keep biting each other's lips as if we are both in a fevered dream, half crazed, desperate with what we know is awaiting us. The same desperation is being portrayed in the moans coming just as fast from our mouths, encouraging the other to unleash their need without shame.

The first drag of the blade's razor edge across his chest pulls a shocked hissing sound of pleasure from him. I watch his eyes close, pulling the air into his lungs with a shiver of release. Even as my eyes remain fixed, my mouth opens to dip my tongue along the red beads beginning to bubble. The spice of him glazes my mouth leaving me wanting more.

"Don't hold back," he coaxes, allowing me to find my own appetite.

Sucking to pull the last bit of blood forward before moving on, I let his moan dance around me. Smiling to myself, I watch as his fists knot the sheets of my bed, bracing for my next stroke of the blade. He loves to make the blade dance across my back, watching me writhe for him. I thirst for him, and I just cut eager to have him flowing into my mouth.

The blade glides along the curve of his stomach, causing the blood to roll from beneath its path. The tension in his body holds for the full length I travel, pulling a straight sound of raw lust from behind his gritted teeth. Hot fluid fills my mouth, forcing me to swallow faster than I normally would like to keep it contained behind my lips. I can hear myself moaning around him as I grind his leg to ease an ache quickly building between my thighs while I drink from the wound I've gladly made on his perfect skin.

Adjusting his leg to better fit my needs. "Keep a pattern, Harper," he commands, his once playful voice, heavy now with our mounting hunger. "Keep a pattern and come for me."

"Not yet," I pant, still hungry for something more. Craving something darker, something unnamed and just as wet as I am.

Jedrek laughs, fisting my hair in his hand to pull my face from his wound. "My hungry girl, it won't be the last time. Just the first. Now, swallow and come."

Diving back to the blood waiting for my mouth, my tongue travels in reverse of the cut I made. Panting from the warmth of my torment, Jedrek's hand massages the back of my head while my hips grind on his thigh. Hearing him, tasting him, having this frustration built inside of me for so long, the first crash hits hard, bowing my back when the waves ride over me. Still, he keeps my head pushed to his stomach, keeping me buried in the blood he bleeds for me. His skin will heal as he wills it, but for now, he wants the sensation of suffering I am providing him even as I fight, despite my own rolling moans, to keep my tongue buried amid the blood pooling around it.

My free hand slips beneath the elastic band of his navy silk boxers when the last of my groaning fades into his skin bringing a deep laugh from above me. He's thick, hard, leaking for me. He's barely contained by such thin cloth. My fingers are greeted with the thick dampness of eagerness to be inside of me. The blood was hot, but this, this is a heat which hurls my body back into throes of a madness for which I have been becoming delirious to drown underneath.

Licking my fingers, I stare up at him, loving how his breaths turn as ragged and uneven as my patience. "Shall we keep going?" I ask him, pushing the blade's tip against where the elastic meets his hip.

Jedrek doesn't speak. His fist in my hair jerks me aside, his other hand is open, demanding the blade from me. Pressure lifts me to my knees before he uses the dagger to slice away my blouse and bra. Shoving me to all fours, pulling my head back to bare my neck, he drags his lips across it as he climbs behind me.

"Don't be scared to scream," he breathes, tightening his grip on my hair pulling it taunt.

Biting down on my neck, he drags his dagger lazily over my upper shoulder in a soft 'S' shape. The razor feeling carves a low protest of pain from me even as I can feel my body relaxing with an almost exhale.

"Such a hungry girl," he moans into the warmth I feel flowing over my skin. "What have you been doing, Harper, to be so hungry for release?"

My body betrays me as it presses against him where he has knelt between my legs when he starts to drink the blood his cut has provided for him. My mouth was greedy on him, on me, his is soft, slow, deliberate to draw me further into desperation. His tongue licks my blood in patterns as if is a topping on a dessert, making sounds of appreciation along the way. I would fall from under the delirium of pleasure if he didn't have a secure hold on my hair.

When my hips become demanding, he whispers against my bleeding skin, "Slow down, Harper. You're not ready yet."

Again, I feel the burning razor slip across my back, lower this time, spinning in a long pattern to pull a soft scream in small bursts as I become breathless. There are no words of encouragement before he bends over me to drink from his handiwork. His hand grips tighter and tighter, straining to maintain control of himself. Jedrek's blood lust grows, pushing against my backside in a pattern matching his speed with his breathing. There's no time in-between before he cuts me again, biting the flesh to pull more blood into his mouth than just the blade has provided for him.

I'm panting, fighting against his fist of restraint as my body twists under his mouth. "Now who needs to slow down?" I moan under his pressing weight.

He laughs, placing the dagger down beside us. "I get carried away once your taste is in my mouth," his voice caresses my back. "You're just so sweet."

"Am I?" I purr.

"Taste wise, at least," Jedrek answers my question with amusement.

He has the lead, but he's letting me decide the pace when his fingers start to ease my slacks down, taking my soaked thong with them. My body might be screaming for him, but he knows at any moment my mind can flip from where we are to where we were just moments ago. He moves so carefully, his hands caressing me with his nonverbal directions to undress. I can smell the scent of my lust as soon as the room's air envelopes the dampness his attention has caused me. That gifted mouth of his teases my exposed skin while helping to free my legs from the clinging fabric in silence, lending his tongue to keep my attention riveted with promises as wet as I am.

"Not yet," he whispers against my hip when my back arches naturally for him. "Just let me enjoy you."

The sounds of frustration dragging from my throat cause him to laugh against my skin. With my head down on the bed, I never saw what his plans were to allow him to enjoy me. It never occurred to me there might be something to his words. I was too lost amid the leisurely patterns of his tongue and the feel of his warm breath inching closer and closer to parts of me weeping with need of his touch. When the dagger's cold metal hilt parts me, the sound of shock and pleasure was torn from me.

My hips which were moving so eagerly a second ago now are ridged, stiff as they wait to see how my body handles being stretched around the metal object.

Jedrek's free hand comes around to slowly trace circles around my heated core, pressing randomly down to keep a maddening unknown pattern and my mind busy. "Relax," he coaxes, removing the hilt its full length before insisting it be replaced inside of me. "Just relax. Let me enjoy you," he moans hotly against my back, "before I enjoy you."

My mind wants to rebel. Some dying need to be seen as that same good little girl filled with decent morals I was before tripping and falling into this world, that last flicker of hope for me, is screaming in the void. Even as I'm listening to myself gasping, moaning, begging for him with each thrust of the hilt reaching deeper inside of me, sliding against the walls of my body with its ridges slapping me with a pattern against his pattern, I'm torn between shame and shattering satisfaction.

"Keep going," he's begging me, almost pleading with me with his own labored breathing. "Please fucking keep going, Harper. You're so beautiful to watch when you just let go."

The sound of my name amid his desperation is my undoing. The first orgasm was a bolt of lightning with soft shocks in wake. This one built slowly, pulling from where the hilt keeps hitting deep inside of me under Jedrek's skilled hand. His maddening circles are a life raft, trying to keep my mind from succumbing to a complete frenzy of uncontrolled movements and sounds as the slow burn erupts inside of me. It rolls me with wave after wave of spine bending tension of pure pleasure until I need him for gravity.

"Jedrek!" I hear his name scream from me, somewhere deep where I keep my darkest secrets.

"Don't stop," he answers his name with the same raw emotions, replacing the hilt with himself pushing my body with a rougher pattern built from his need for his own release.

I didn't need his encouragement to match his speed with my hips meeting his, but when his hands tightly gripped mine to slam them against his body I could do nothing but moan in agreement. Hearing his vocal shouts with each connection is driving me from my head. I'm pure nerves, lost in every sensation he's ripping through my body, pushing me further and further out of my cage I have built around myself these past few weeks.

"Let them go, Harper," he's grunting between thrusts. "Just let it all go," he's commanding, coaxing, pleading, anything to bring me to full release not just sexually but emotionally, too.

As each of his moans become a higher pitch his pattern begins to dissolve into a hurried frenzy. Soon the warmth of him will be flowing into me, coating me just as his voice will be covering my body.

"Harper. Harper. Harper." Jedrek keeps moaning hitting my body when my name slips from his lips. "Please, now. Please," he pleads with me. "Give the souls to me. Come with me."

His pleading tone destroys me, exploding what I thought were the strong bars of my cage, sending me over the ledge with screams of release as I let everything go from within me. Every argument these last few weeks have held, every job gone wrong for whatever reason, every soul which has refused to leave me and return to their place of holding, every emotion I've refused to name, or place, I scream into the pillow with my release making us both slippery wet with his final strokes as he pumps his own release into mine.

"That was beautiful," a male voice crashes over us both, tearing Jedrek from me abruptly, leaving more than just my body chilled with his sudden departure.

Turning my head to stare over my shoulder I watch as the tall male begins to clap in approval of the show he just witnessed without our knowing. Lucifer, without an expression upon his beautiful face, arrived just as Jedrek had warned he would.

Lucifer is still clapping when Jedrek kneels before him, nude and still fighting to collect his breath. The taller man is dressed as richly as I remember him from our first meeting. The pressed red shirt as dark as sins is tucked into black slacks flowing down to shoes polished to shine like black scrying mirrors. He's beautiful, but evil has to be that way. It's easy to fall for the 'good guys'. The dangerous ones have to override that sense of self-preservation somehow. We can buy our own cookies these days, but vibrators will never look this damn good.

"I sent you to discover where my souls are, Jedrek," Lucifer's deep voice vibrates through my room as I slide under my sheets with as much nonchalant as my panic will allow, "not discover how loud you could make her scream."

"I've been louder," I mutter with some weird sense of a bruised ego.

Jedrek tilts his head slightly to look at me over his shoulder before telling his master from his knelt position, "I have the souls, Lord Lucifer."

Lucifer tilts his head to stare down at his kneeling general. "And?"

"They taste of magic, but not hers," Jedrek explains. "It's too fragmented, brittle. They're held together by such weak bindings they're collapsing in on themselves."

Lucifer peers at me, again. I feel as if the sheet is suddenly too thin with how he is staring, but I refuse to squirm under his gaze.

"Or perhaps," Lucifer muses, eyes traveling the outline of my body, "you're too blinded by her. I can see how she might manipulate you."

"I am not so easy to manipulate." Jedrek's cold voice cuts me sharper than his dagger.

"You feel no loyalty to your witch?" Lucifer asks with skepticism. "You feel no need to keep that body alive for yourself?"

Jedrek's head lowers further, telling the man, "My loyalty has been, and will always be, to you, Lucifer. I fought with you. I fell with you. I remain with you, my lord."

"Then give me the souls," Lucifer toys with him, testing him to see what he'll do.

I watch as Jedrek stands to stare into Lucifer's eyes. My room falls into an almost unnatural silence of tension while the two peer at the other. This battle is about me, but it's not my battle. Jedrek has been surviving in this world before it even came to be made. He was one of God's long before he became one of Lucifer's, and if anyone knows how to manage both sides, it's him.

There's nothing verbally exchanged between the two men. Jedrek simply slides his hands up the body of his master, bringing his palms to rest on the chest of the slightly taller man before tilting his head to rest his lips upon the mouth of Lucifer. I watch them slowly grow bolder with each other from where I seem to have been forgotten on my bed. When Lucifer embraces him, it's only the sound of Jedrek's moan which covers the sound of my ragged inhale.

The two men begin to devour each other's mouths. Eyes closed, bodies pressed tightly together it becomes a match of moans and tongues as each ignites the other's fire. I'm watching them both silently, unaware my hand has slid down my stomach to touch myself, stirring my own fires which are still slick from the man bringing heat back to my room with his unquenchable lust.

"Can you taste her?" Jedrek asks Lucifer's mouth.

Lucifer moans his reply. "Yes."

"And the souls?" Jedrek asks, again.

"So many lost to me," Lucifer bemoans, voice a cocktail of pleasure and suffering.

"But not from her," Jedrek whispers, rubbing his cheek against Lucifer's while watching me.

He hasn't missed my hand exploring the depths of myself while I watched the two of them. His eyebrow is arched high in a question as my back slightly arches under the pleasure of my fingers and the weight of the light in his amused eyes. When his finger's trace the outline of Lucifer's swollen cock my mouth opens as my breath catches in my throat.

"Your witch might not be the one, but it's a witch just the same, Jedrek," Lucifer reprimands, "and the witches I trust to you to keep in line."

"Let me show you my penance." Jedrek's voice might sound humbled, but the part of his face not buried into his master's cheek is smirking at me with his eyes glowing with his lust as he watches my fingers dance faster and faster from behind the bent leg blocking Lucifer's view.

With an expertise I will never own, Jedrek undoes the zipper of Lucifer's slacks with a slow ease, sliding his flattened hand into them. My eyes are darting from that flattened palm to Lucifer's relaxing face, to Jedrek's amused face and back to that palm with an element of fear I might miss something, something I may never have a chance to enjoy again. His hand grasps the thickened shaft pulling it free from the confines of the pressed slacks and pulling a gasp from me before I can recover from the sight.

"You don't mind the witch watching, do you?" Jedrek asks as his body starts to melt down the side of Lucifer.

Lucifer merely shakes his head, pushing gently on Jedrek's shoulder to further guide him into the position we all know he's headed towards.

Jedrek doesn't wait until he's fully on his knees before taking the other man into his mouth. There is no gentle teasing this time from Jedrek. No sliding of his tongue, or caressing of his lips to bring his master an early taste of what is to become him. He dives quickly into his goal of bringing his master to spilling his cum into his mouth.

The speed of which Jedrek is sliding his mouth along the length of the ridged shaft has caused me to subconsciously match the pattern with my own fingers sliding in and out of myself. He encourages Lucifer to fuck his mouth when he wraps his arms around the other man's body and pulls it forward when he swallows the entire length of him. Their tempo is rough, almost brutal with an edge of pain to it, when Lucifer takes over, forcing Jedrek to either keep up or choke.

Both are moaning in different pitches, different reasons, different manner, but moaning in increasing symphonies of male triumph. Jedrek is about to bring both of us to spilling over when he dares Lucifer to still be the dominant one by increasing his speed, yet again, and it's the exact step that causes his master to lose the battle.

Lucifer's body becomes ridged with only small little movements in his hips as his moaning changes from the shortened almost grunt like tempo he was keeping to elongated strained sounds. "Don't swallow, yet," he fights to say between the sounds fighting to free themselves from his throat. "Don't you fucking swallow a single bit of it."

I watch as Jedrek struggles with this command. He's brought his hand to help finish the final strokes allowing him to focus on just the head of the slick shaft, sucking, and pulling on the tender pink flesh to hold everything spilling forth from it. Soft, wet sounds finish the oral fucking Jedrek has provided as he slowly slides his mouth free, making sure to keep his lips sealed to keep every drop safe.

"Now go finish your witch," Lucifer commands with a smirk that makes my heart jolt around in the walls of my ribs. "Let my cum slip from your mouth onto her pussy then eat her. She better fucking scream, Jedrek."

I'm already screaming internally. Watching them silently, frozen, and hoping I was forgotten was one thing. Now the center of their attention is a different stage I'm not sure I want to be a part of or sure I know where it will lead. Jedrek has no limits when it comes to sex and I'm sure the King of Hell has most likely invented the limits. I don't even know my limits. Times like this I wish I had that whole safe word thing.

Jedrek stalks towards me with the same amused eyes watching me. I know he can see my fear telegraphed across my face adding more eagerness to his very erect shaft which has to be aching from being ignored. My eyes are locked on his. I don't know who pulled the thin sheet from my body. Nor do I know which one of them removed my frozen hand from my previous exploring attempts. I'm paralyzed, merely only able to watch him climb between my legs with his eyes solid on mine to keep me grounded in this moment.

I know Lucifer has come to stand beside us. I can feel his presence without having to turn to physically look to see him. His hand is playing with Jedrek's black hair with a sharp edge of discipline to remind him of his commands. It's only when Jedrek is hovering right over my swollen lips from the previous abuse and my own torture to them does he finally break our eye contact. Slowly, so slowly he opens his mouth to let the collection slide from between his perfectly sculpted lips onto my waiting flesh. It glazes over the pink skin, adding a shine which for some reason erupts a moan from me as I watch it roll down his chin.

"Finish her," Lucifer's deep voice rolls out his command.

Just as before, Jedrek dives into his work, skipping the gentle entrance he normally prides himself on. I normally love watching him enjoy me but his furiosity has snapped my neck backwards and has me screaming under the rage of his mouth and tongue. He is sucking, and alternating slapping the most tender parts of me with the warm, trained tongue of his. I can't catch my breath fast enough to keep up with the sounds he's forcing me to make or keep my body still as it fights on its own to escape from the hot torment, he's putting me through.

Lucifer has taken Jedrek's shaft into his hand at some point while I was staring at the ceiling screaming for my life. His eyes are devouring the scene before him. His breath is following the tempo of his hand stroking Jedrek. He's moaning deep in his chest as he's leaning over to be able to reach around. His attention is causing Jedrek to moan as his face is buried deep inside of me, vibrating against my sensitive flesh causing me to bounce under his added sensations.

"Make your witch come," I watch Lucifer whisper into Jedrek's ear. "I want her to scream for you."

Jedrek takes the command as a challenge, alternating brutal suction with agonizing pauses, teasing me until I'm sobbing, begging. He ups the pressure, sucking on me to the point of me being afraid I might explode only to let off right as I start to fight against his hands holding me down, only to start again and again and again. He twists, licks, bites—driving me higher, tighter, until release explodes, my body arching violently as I scream for him with my release when the pressure finally builds to sweet pleasure as it bounces my whole upright body balancing on my arms with it's escape.

In my haze, I can hear Jedrek's own moans, feeling his body slide on my legs where he has been kneeling. A hand is massaging warmth into my thighs, and I know it's Lucifer placing Jedrek's cum on me from where he was stroking him just a moment ago. Normally I would protest, but I don't have the voice or even the air in my lungs to form the words.

"Now when you go to find out what is happening to my souls you will wear the scent of me and your accomplice in your failures to me, Harper," Lucifer tells me. "Fix my soul problem, or my hounds will find you. Reeking of our sex, they will hunt you down swiftly."

"So, no shower?" I ask, fighting for breath. "Got it."

Jedrek bites my thigh where he still has his head hiding as a warning to 'shut the fuck up'.

"With this much cum on you, Harper," Lucifer laughs, "you will need more than a shower to confuse my hounds. Even the most basic of demons could find you like this."

I feel my face scrunch and hear myself say before I can stop my suicidal ways, "Did you just call me a cum dumpster?"

Lucifer leans close, whispering against my ear, "I said you smell like one. What you become is still up to you. But you're off to a promising start."

He fades, leaving only the chill of his absence and the wreckage of my self-esteem. His words detonate every buried moral landmine I've been avoiding since stepping into their world. Somewhere deep inside, the little girl who once dreamed of husbands, white picket fences, and children curls up and tries not to cry.

"I feel gross."

I squirm inside my clothes standing in the kitchen with the after sex munchies. Jedrek had refused showers, claiming it was pointless and would most likely only anger Lucifer if he was still watching us. He said there were worse things than walking around with the remnants of the after sex stuck to us. This was where I reminded him that demons are liars.

Jedrek smiles at me, already collected and back to his sexually mischievous self. "You don't smell gross."

I wrinkle my nose at him as my stomach twists with the thought he is standing across from me, leaning on the counter inhaling the memories of what just happened. "That's gross."

"You're acting like a child," he teases, smirk unwavering.

"No, I'm not," I say defensively, clutching an extra large bag of cheese puffs like a shield with my orange powder covered fingers. "I just don't see a reason to talk about what just happened."

"Your eyes when he and I touched suggest otherwise," he mocks, prying at my comfort zone.

With a mouth full of cheese like cardboard, I shrug. "Just didn't know you like men."

"I like sex," he replies without hesitation, his tone flat but laced with dark promise. "I like the power it gives me over people."

"Power?" I scoff, wiping orange streaks on my jeans. Who cares about stains when your thighs are glazed like doughnuts? "You're good, but maybe check the ego."

Jedrek chuckles softly. "When you hit that peak, even your walls come down. For those few seconds, I can see everything you're hiding from me. I know every secret, every lie, every goal. Even your childhood is a book to be read if I want to look that deep. It's how I can take the souls you keep locked away who refuse to return. It's that way with everyone. Even him."

"You do that?" I whisper, an unexplained ache blooming in my chest.

Jedrek straightens, fishing his keys from his pocket, pretending to be distracted. "Not anymore," he murmurs, as if admitting too much. "Besides, it's more fun to just see what trouble you drag us into these days."

He smiles at me, a smile I know is costing him something he doesn't normally spend out of fear he may come up empty handed. For once it doesn't reach his eyes. They stay dull, waiting, prepared for the fall.

I do the only thing I can think to do. The thing I have secretly been wanting to do for a few days now, but my pride wouldn't let me. I quickly walk over to where he stands, and crash into his chest, letting him enfold me into his arms. He kisses me, using only his lips. Softly pulling my bottom lip with his slowly into his mouth to release it and repeat. It's so gentle, tender that I sigh against him.

"Oh, my littlest witch," he murmurs into my hair. "What am I going to do with you?"

I sigh again, but out of defeat not due to his gentle touching of my face and hair. "That thing with your tongue was nice," I suggest. Mostly as a joke. Somewhere as a joke. Basically, because sarcasm is my go to shield when feeling too exposed as I do right now.

"I'll keep that in mind," he whispers into my curls. "I'm sure the cuts, even as thin as they are, still burn."

"Only when I move a certain way," I admit to his chest where I have buried my head.

"Then let's not move that way while we figure out how to collect the rest of the souls," he suggests as if I'm a small child.

"Yes, Daddy," I mutter, dripping sarcasm.

He chuckles low, the sound rumbling against me. "Careful. That's a game we've yet to play."

Reactively, I shrink further into the hollow of his chest. "My mistake."

His fingers are trailing up and down my spine as he holds me. "The souls are obviously whole when you summon them or else we would have noticed them having problems in their bodies," he muses into my red curls.

Nodding, I add, "Or interacting with their families."

"So there is something blocking their return," he muses against my hair.

Tilting my head against his chest, I tell him, "That would be the ground itself. There has to be some kind of barrier that for some reason isn't allowing a complete return."

"Why though?" he asks, while holding me. "Why would someone only want part of a soul and not the whole soul?"

"The whole soul missing would be noticed much quicker. Little pieces here and there would allow someone to collect their power slowly, but safer," I reason as someone who would be scared to poke Heaven and Hell with a giant stick. Then another thought hits me, "Why isn't Gabrielle down here adding to the death threats?"

Jedrek shrugs, but I know he knows. "Maybe you've summoned more of ours as lately than theirs."

"Lucky me" I answer him, knowing he's lying but I'm not going to push it.

"The Coven is gone though. I would know if they were back or hiding even." His fingers toy with my curls as his chest rumbles with his thoughts. "This has to be rouge witches trying their hand at some kind of occult garbage they read on the back of some pagan self-help book."

"It would have to be happening at the cemetery. They would need to be at the location to put the barrier down." I tell his black shirt, wondering how I'm going to explain to him I forgot to put the bag away before running to him.

"It's a big area to cover with a barrier spell," he's still using my curls as a muse.

I shrug, trying to play off my attempts to remove the orange powder streaks from his shirt. "Depends how the spell is worked.

I know he knows this. He knows more about witches than I do. He has been watching witches since he fell with Lucifer. It's his main duty. I always imagined it's not the 'devil' that tempts women, as the old, scared men swear. It's always been him. Lucifer seems a little too nonchalant about mortals to care about meeting a bunch of half-clad women in forests for orgies. Jedrek though. Half-naked women high out of their minds and horny seem something he would very much be very chalant.

"You already know this though." I leave it between a question and a statement.

"Maybe," he concedes, pulling the red mess away from my face. "Maybe I just like the fact you're letting me hold you and don't want to rush this."

"Even though we are on a timer against some demon puppies?" I remind him.

Jedrek lifts one shoulder while running his fingers along my neck. "I keep spare virgins for when he threatens me with them."

"Jedrek," I squeak before I can stop my outrage causing him to laugh outright.

"Fine. Let's go see if we can find some secondhand witches," Jedrek runs the strand of hair he has in hand under his nose closing his eyes while he inhales the scent of the curl trying it best to wrap itself around his fingers like ivy.

"Sure," I whisper, watching him, remembering this man I'm curled up to isn't human at all.

It's easy to forget what he truly is when he's holding me like this, being gentle and tender with me. It's easy to forget how easily he could kill me, hurt me, or even torture me for no other reason than it might amuse him. Jedrek isn't even his true name. It's the name he tells mortals to call him, hiding who he is behind the skin he is wearing and now I have to confess his expensive black shirt is covered in powdered cheese.

"Uh, Jedrek," I stall, stuttering on how to tell a killer I messed his shirt up.

"Hmmm?" the soft sound comes from his throat as cool colored blue eyes open to stare at me.

"I got cheese powder on your shirt," I flow the words too fast together. I sound like a toddler confessing to a crime.

He nods. "I know."

"You do?" I don't know whether to exhale or start running.

"Mmmhmm," he nods.

"Oh. Well, it's not too bad." I tug the bag free and place it on the counter.

"When the killing starts it's this I will find myself thinking about," he tells me with honest amusement. "I will ask myself, *"Self, how is it this woman who was just covered in manufactured cheese powder is tearing the heads from bodies with a smile?""*

"I'm sure there are a lot of people who ask themselves a question similar to that," I tell him, using a kitchen towel to dust the front of his shirt.

Grabbing my hands to stop me, he takes the towel to bring my knuckles to his lips, grazing them while looking into my eyes.

"Thank you," he whispers against my skin. "Thank you," he repeats again before looking for his keys where he had placed them on the counter from earlier.

Then he releases me, snatching his keys off the counter. He arches his brows with a boyish grin before spinning out of the kitchen with his usual flair. Our moment has passed. Jedrek is back to being himself, his armor for the outside world has been replaced. Just like my sarcasm, he flirts, smiles, and lets those boyish charms disarm his enemies. Sometimes I think the world was a better place when we could all walk around with giant swords and shields. At least those were honest walls instead of the walls we have had to construct to protect ourselves.

The chances of just stumbling upon them here are going to be pretty slim," I say out loud, but I might as well as be talking to myself or to the many rows of cement markers we have been traveling down. Jedrek doesn't slow his step despite the defeat in my tone.

The late night air is still holding the summer humidity. How air can cling to skin and clothes is something I have never figured out, but it is, almost becoming alive in a way that makes creepy men seem almost welcoming to be around this time of year. Or how the very thing you need to breathe can take your breath away as soon as you step outside like a cruel joke, but it does, every season and yet none of this is bothering the man ahead of me as I struggle to keep my mood slightly above neutral. I really think monsters miss their true recruitment pointers. If they only could focus better, really narrow down on their true bonus features to turning to their side, their ranks would double over night.

"You'd be amazed at how easy it is to catch stupid people," he calls back to me. "Mostly because stupid people never think they will get caught."

"And you think we are just going to what, stumble on some giant spell circle or something?" I mock.

"You really are a behind in your craft," he mocks in return. "A circle would limit the spell. Something like this needs an area for offerings. It has to be a set location each time, something that wouldn't be disturbed."

"Mausoleums," I whisper as the idea comes to me.

"Exactly," he agrees.

The mausoleums are in the back of the cemetery. Their large gothic architectures always loom over the garden of the dead like mini castles holding their families secure inside their stone structures. Family names are carved in scrolling fonts or bold blocks, boasting of their prestige. Normally these buildings are locked for privacy. Where as normally a blind eyes is given to the cemetery for all the extra activity that the local houses hold here, but this would be sloppy to allow unhoused witches to have open access to so many souls.

"Destroy their altar. Break the spell. Everything returns to normal. Go home and take a shower. Seems easy enough." I'm pulling on each door I come to hoping one of these giant, overpriced death hotels will open.

Jedrek laughs. "It's never that simple, Harper. You should know that by now."

Frustrated, sticky in more ways than one, and in more ways than I'd like to admit even to myself, tired, and over all of this, I turn to where he is leaning against a giant cross in a way too cliché pose. "What the fuck does that mean?"

"It means they are in the middle one right now," he tells me with a wink.

The laugh that escapes me is one of complete irony and exasperation. "Of course they are. Why would something be simple? Why would we just be able to swoosh in and smush something? Why would life let us just skadoodle out of just one death threat?"

Jedrek's head tilts as I ramble. "Harper? When have you last slept?"

"What day is it?" I ask honestly.

"I see." Jedrek pushes himself from the stone cross the way he does as if gravity doesn't exist for him. "Let me take the lead on this one? I don't want you hexing the wrong one in there. Like me."

"I'm not *that* tired," I hiss at him as he passes me.

He lifts one eyebrow at me with doubt but says nothing when he enters the structure carved with the giant name declaring it claimed for the Gardy family.

The smell of abandonment collides with me, invoking blocked memories of visiting my own mother in her grave. For a moment, my heart can't find a rhythm as the scent pulls me into my own past. The many candles flicker their flames from our entrance, almost pointing the way for us, giving us little clues as to where the invaders to the tomb's many sleepers are hiding. Little golden plaques seem to be staring at me, declaring those inside belong to them and not for my meddling. The whole entrance feels as if it's holding its breath to see why we have come, like we are being watched somehow.

"It doesn't feel right," I whisper, hugging myself.

"No, it doesn't," Jedrek stills, slipping from the playful playboy to predator.

Whatever I am sensing, he is tracking. This is how I know my sense of self-preservation has completely disappeared. A normal person upon seeing a demon becoming worried would think this would be where they need to leave. If something from Hell is concerned, maybe a mortal should just run? Nope. I follow behind him like a bad Scooby-Do side kick into danger.

His walk has no sound. Nor does his movement disturb the candles. Which is fine because I sound like I'm leading a whole school of small children a on field trip touring exhibits. My nerves were fried before we arrived. The building tension of 'hey guess what's around every alcove' isn't doing the last few I have working any favors. I'm bumping into every standing ornate candle display despite them being placed right in front of my face. Jedrek is having to catch them last minute. Eventually he does it without having to turn his head, expecting me to bumper car off of each one.

It's a moaning sound that reaches me first telling me we aren't alone. It's low and soft. My soul prays it's not one of pain, that we are not about to stumble across a scene of human sacrifice. A vessel to hold the souls would be needed for this type of workings, something alive to feed the fragments until they are needed. Something like a living jar to hold them would make sense in such a case of this type of magic. A human branded with their seal to collect and keep the energy for them. They would not release them without some form of feeding.

Just like Jedrek does during sex with me. He has to pull them free from where I have unconsciously locked them tightly away to keep them separate from my day-to-day life. If that is the case, this has become so much more than either of us thought it might be. A human vessel will need to be pulled apart and eventually, sadly killed to be fully freed from their grasp.

The moans grows louder the closer the back alcove comes into view. The candles have changed from the basic white, to red, and then black in a pattern that holds answers only to those who have placed them. The smoke of heavy herbs fills the air heavily here. Some of them I think I might know but most are too blended in the air and too complicated to pick apart. They are just becoming part of the heavy feel surrounding me.

There is something familiar about it all. The way the smoke is dancing. The way the herbs are calling to a part of me, a dark part of me boxed and stored away. I know this ritual. I know I know it because of the dread I am feeling as I turn this last corner. I know what is ahead of us. I know what we are about to see because I have seen it before when I was little. Like an old, grainy VHS tape, the memory plays of my mother and the two men I watched from my bedroom window. I know this ritual because my mother taught me it one fall afternoon without her knowing she had showed me.

"Jedrek," I whisper, "don't."

He slightly turns towards me from his slowed walk. "Why?"

"I know this ritual," I explain, trying to not choke on the words strangling my throat.

He smiles with a wink, "Me too."

He takes my hand, pulling us both to the edge of the last barrier between me and a childhood nightmare. True to memory, there it is. Everything from the night I remember of my mother is playing out before me in full color. The woman even looks the same with dark hair and a white cotton night gown, pushed high above her back to allow the man behind her access to her body. A half mask of white with painted red symbols covers all of her facial features as she takes the other man deep into her mouth. She's bent high, her back arched to give the man behind her full, unrelenting access.

The white mask with its painted symbols hides her face, but it can't hide the way her lips are stretching wide as she chokes down the cock in front of her. She braces against the man behind her, his grip forcing her forward, driving her deeper onto the thick length that bulges her throat. Each thrust from behind shoves her mouth further down, gagging her on the massive shaft until drool spills over her chin. Her moans are guttural, broken around the cock stretching her to her limit, yet she keeps the rhythm, her body shuddering as both men use her in perfect, brutal sync.

Both men are dressed in black robes as they ride her each with their own brutal rhythm. Their white deer skull masks with golden painted horns cover all of their features. They seem oblivious to each other, petting and praising the woman for how good she is doing while taking care of them. It's then I noticed their gloved hands with gold nails sharpened to tips as claws. Unlike my mother who was a chosen vessel. This woman is just an offering. All she has been chosen for tonight is to raise the energy for the ritual.

The question gnawing at me is whether she even knows what she's being used for in all of this. And if she doesn't, then where is the true vessel for this spell? Do I care? Not in the slightest. All I want is a hard drink before this nightmare begins for me. Is that really too much to ask? Just one fucking drink?

The woman is arching, her spine bending to give the man behind her every possible angle of entry as he growls for her to relax, to open for him. His voice is rough, vibrating through the air as he shifts his weight and drags her into a new position. The movement forces a scream from her throat, muffled by the little space left in her mouth.

From this vantage, I see all of him. He's thick, hard, and glistening with her wetness as he pulls free, only to slide back into her body with a slow, deliberate thrust. The candlelight glints off the slick surface of his length, each vein, each ridge outlined by the many candles around us. My stomach knots, my body tightening in an instinctive clench at the thought of what she must be enduring to take him so deep. The sheer stretch, the way she keeps arching trying to accommodate him, sends a shiver racing through me of pity and envy.

His head tilts backward, the hollow deer skull with its long antlers fixed on the ceiling's painted tiles like a grotesque idol. He moans through the mask, guttural and broken, the sound distorted as if coming from somewhere less than human. His hands grip her hips, holding her higher than she could ever raise herself, keeping her body suspended in the air, completely in his control.

His rhythm is unhurried, cruel in its slowness. Each exaggerated stroke is dragged out, savoring every inch of her tight, wet body as though the act itself is the ritual. Every withdrawal reveals him glistening more than before, soaked in her arousal until he shines obscenely in the firelight. The shadows carve the ridges of him sharper, more defined, forcing me to see what I couldn't in the dark before.

My mouth may be becoming dry as I watch, but I am not. Heat and unease is twisting inside me. A duet of shame and need. The air is thick with melted wax, herbs and sweat. The sound of him sliding into her echoing over the low, ragged groans behind the mask. I should look away, but I can't. I want to. Mother help me. I want to, but I just can't.

"That's a horrible way to give a blow job," Jedrek voice pulls me back to reality.

I can feel my cheeks start to burn with shame as I force my eyes away from the couple. "What?" I force my tongue to form.

"Look at her," he motions to the front of the chain.

The dark-haired woman is on her knees, lips straining around the other masked man's cock as he slowly rides her face with a measured rhythm. Her movements are slow, halting, the struggle written in every tremor of her jaw as she forces herself to take more of his length, to stretch wider than she should be able to. The thickness of him is cruel, and yet she keeps trying despite what her jaw will allow her to accommodate. She is so terribly desperate to please him.

His hands cradle her head so gently in a stark contrast to the male behind her. His claws tipped in gold tracing the edges of her face like a parody of tenderness. The hollow sockets of the deer skull stare down at her, patient, predatory. He doesn't thrust forward, doesn't slam into her throat. He waits, perfectly still, except for the subtle, random movements of his hips, he is letting her choke and gag around him at her own pace. It's as if the pleasure lies not in his using of her, but in his watching of her offering herself up piece by piece until there's nothing left. Soaking not only himself in her mouth but in her suffering.

Her moans vibrate against him, wet and desperate, spilling around the thick length that blocks her cries. Each sound from her tightens the forbidden knot inside of me. They reverberate in my chest until I can almost feel his phantom weight at the back of my own throat. His claws flex and relax against her cheeks in time with her struggle, as though he's savoring the moment, waiting to see if she'll either give in or fail entirely.

Compared to the brutal rhythm of the man behind her, this scene should feel less erotic. But it doesn't. It feels so much more in ways I cannot explain to myself.

The restraint, the patience, the control of it all seeps under my skin. It unsettles me more than the violence. And worse, much worse, it stirs something sharp and hot low in my belly. A jealousy I can't explain. A shameful ache I can't ignore. I want to look away. I don't. But I'm telling myself I want to.

"What about her?" my dry mouth struggles to whisper to him.

Jedrek makes a tsking sound. "No one does a blowjob like that."

"Are you really critiquing her?" I ask, trying to hide my hungry stares.

"If they are going to do sex magic at least do the sex right," Jedrek whispers his complaint with a little too much spice to his voice. "She's mostly choking and struggling. Where is the skill level?"

"I don't think it's the sex that matters," I tell him pointing to the gloved claws doing my best to not look at what is really taking place. "I think the sex is just to raise the energy. Doesn't really matter how it's done, you jerk. They are going to kill her."

"Of course they are going to kill her," he sighs as if I'm the slowest person in the room and maybe I am. "They need her blood right as they finish to mix with their semen."

"Both of them?" I ask, watching the man in the back appear to be much closer than the man in the front.

The man in the back has abandoned his restraint. His hips snap harder, faster, driving into her with a hunger that refuses to be ignored. Each thrust is deeper than the last. He is punishing her, unrelenting, as though he means to carve himself into her body until she is nothing but a sheath for his need. The force of his movements fans the tiny black and red flames scattered around the cement floor. The candlelight is sputtering as wax bleeds from their glass prisons in thick, dripping streams like foreshadowing to what is about to happen.

Every stroke rips another sound from him. His moans dragging raw through his throat. They are guttural and heavy. He is torn between control and surrender. He is fighting the inevitable rush, desperate to hold it off and yet aching to be consumed by it. His grip on her hips is merciless, fingers biting into flesh, locking her in place so she can't move, can't escape, can't even breathe without his permission. To him, she exists only for this moment, only for their ritual. A body. A vessel. Nothing more.

And yet, as I watch him take her like this, watching the raw pleasure quake through him as he loses himself in her, disgust coils inside me. My gut twists with it, knowing they are going to kill her as soon as they are done. So why are my thighs clenching with something else? Something I don't want to admit.

She is faceless, nameless, stripped of everything but her body, and still, I feel the sting of envy. Envy that she is the one pinned beneath him. Envy that he is spilling this need into her, while I can only watch from the shadows. Envy that she is free to enjoy her body with such abandonment.

Jedrek shrugs continuing to watch the three from our hidden vantage point. "Would be overkill," he whispers, "but I wouldn't mind watching both of them finish."

"Seriously," I hiss, his comment bringing me back to the situation and away from the situation, "what is wrong with you?"

"It's been a dry month so far," he offers as his answer. "Just because I'm a demon doesn't mean I don't have needs," he mocks, trying to sound wounded I even dared to ask him.

" Are we just going to let them kill her?" I try not to screech but the whisper still sounds something close to a barn owl's attempt to keep a secret. "So, you can watch two guys have a money shot in deer skulls?"

My temper grows further watching him take his time to contemplate my question.

"I will fucki-" I start before he reaches behind him to place a hand on my leg to settle me.

"Easy there," he whispers. "If you want me to save the fetish dip shit, I'll save the fetish dip shit, but I'm warning you, women like that will just find another dumb way to die."

"But not tonight," I sigh. "Just not while I could have done something to have stopped it."

"Great," he voices his agitation under his breath, "I don't get to watch them finish and we'll most likely end up seeing this idiot again. Yay us."

Since I am behind him, I can see it without needing to see the change. His blue eyes lose their vivid hue, paling into the icy shade that always signals danger. The playful arch of his brows is gone, the smirk erased, the teasing curve of his lips replaced with something sharp, something meant to disarm right before the strike.

It's as though invisible strings pull him upright, or as if he is shadow given flesh. Jedrek rises to his full height, unfolding with predatory grace until he's leaning, casual as ever, against the wall that separates the alcove from the chamber. He waits there, poised, a blade sheathed in stillness, daring them to notice him.

But the men don't. Or maybe they do and just don't care. They are too consumed by their ritual. The heat of it, the bloodlust and the rhythm of their bodies rutting into her have their complete attention. Their thrusts grow harsher, their moans breaking into guttural snarls that no longer sound entirely human.

The air was already thick with sex and sweat and blood and wax, but now there is a new weight. Something in me twists tight, a certainty forming cold and sharp in my chest. We are already too late.

I'm moving before I even realize it, magic ripping out of me, born from fear and urgency, a wild surge I can't hold back. But Jedrek is faster. His arms wrap around me, locking me to his chest as the scream tears from my throat. A scream she will never be allowed to make.

The golden claws slash clean through her neck, the wet sound sharp and final. Her body jerks, blood spraying in a hot rush as the man behind her forces himself free from her. He spills himself on her back in thick, pale ropes, each burst obscene in its timing with her neck, mixing sex and death until I can't tell where one ends and the other begins.

The echoes of his moans both muffled and monstrous behind the bone mask fill the chamber, vibrating against the stone, drowning out everything else but my memory playing out in time behind my eyes with what is playing before my eyes.

The other man is catching the torrent of blood in a golden chalice. His claws hold her limp head up by a fistful of dark hair, tilting her ruined throat so the flow pours cleanly into the cup. His face is tilted with fascination, the same twisted tenderness he showed her before only now she's nothing but an emptied vessel dangling in his grasp.

She was never a woman to them. Never a person. Just a body to be used, a throat to be cut, a sacrifice for their ritual. A faceless, nameless tool.

Jedrek holds me pinned against him, his grip iron even as I thrash in outrage, desperate to tear free. My fury is useless against him. All I can do is watch.

The men never turn, never so much as flicker a glance our way. They move with a sickening calm, as though what they've done is nothing more than procedure. Their hands sweep across her body, gathering the thick semen from her back and mixing it with the blood in the chalice. Seed and sacrifice, life and death, stirred together like a recipe older than time.

They move in silence, redressing piece by piece, the robes falling back into place as though the ritual never happened. The one holding the chalice bends to retrieve the mask from her lifeless face, lifting it free with a reverence that makes bile rise in my throat.

Her features are exposed at last, pale and slack in death, hair dark and tangled with blood. The sight of her knocks the breath from me because now she isn't just a body. She's a person. A woman. And still, to them, she is nothing more than a vessel.

The two men stand slowly, side by side, the chalice glinting in the one's hand. And only then, only when they are ready, they turn. Their masks are tilted toward us as if admitting what they knew all along. That we've been standing here, watching them, and they didn't give a damn.

"Hello, Jedrek," the one holding the chalice says knocking the floor from underneath me, "we were wondering when you would show."

Jedrek shifts me to one arm, still tucking me close to his body to keep me from escaping his grasp to do something stupid. "I was busy with a witch, or I would have been here sooner," he shrugs with the shoulder available to be moved.

"Well, now that you are here," he begins without the least bit of tremble to his voice under the heavy gaze of Jedrek, "how shall we handle this?"

"You're going to fucking die," I hiss, staring at the dead woman's delicate features, wondering why her.

The man notices where I am staring, looking over his shoulder through the eyes of the deer skull, he glances at the corpse before turning back to me. They have painted around their eyes black to hide them amid the skull, but I can see the gentle brown coloring of his as he blinks, watching me, gazing with more than just human skill.

"Don't feel for her," he tells me. "She wanted this."

"Told you so," Jedrek whispers a bit too loudly into my ear.

"What are you two?" I ask, with his eyes churning my insides while under his gaze.

"Wraiths," Jedrek answers for them. "And this is going to hurt," he warns me, hinting of what is to come for us shall we decide to follow the path I have chosen.

"What's a wraith?" I ask, knowing I shouldn't. I should just nod and prepare to have my ass kicked, but no, my mouth always moves before my brain can engage.

The wraith with the chalice tilts his head, and I know he's wondering how does a necromancer not know such a thing. Self-consciously I hide my fingertips with fear they might still have cheese powder on them.

"They are ghosts someone summoned to reanimate a corpse but lost control of for some reason," Jedrek explains with a mock of a whisper. "Now they are free to make our lives a shit show and they often do."

"Well, that's unfair," the speaking one says as if wounded. "We lived by your rules once. Now we just simply don't want to."

"Well," Jedrek sighs, releasing me with a twirl, "Lucifer doesn't seem to care what you want."

"Oh, dear," he says. "Have we gone and pissed off your Daddy? Well, you're right. That is bad."

"I guess the chances of you putting the cup down and just going with Jedrek to explain to Daddy why you've been bad and how sorry you are isn't real high, are they?" I ask, still confused about exactly what is happening, but really not wanting to know much more, but still unable to shut up.

"Sorry," he says. "We have a vessel to feed. She tends to get cranky if her cravings are not met regularly."

"And I guess she likes her blood a little extra salt?" I hear myself ask and even as I hear it, I'm scolding myself, wondering why I am like this. Just why?

"And a good fuck," he tells me, and I can hear the smile behind the mask even if I can't see it.

"Yeah, we are going to have to kill her," Jedrek sighs. "You two know you can't keep pets. It's against the lease agreement."

"You really want to do this, Jedrek?" Deer boy asks.

Jedrek shakes his head with a soft chuckle. "Nope, but you've been naughty, Mezzel. Now, I have to spank you and your mute buddy there."

My nerves fire before I can stop them, and the green smoke answers without hesitation coiling up from within me, alive, instinctual. The tendrils curl around my legs, climbing higher, winding tight as though they are a lover shielding me, possessive and unyielding in their need to keep me safe, stalking the danger ahead of me.

The air hums with their presence. Strands of my red hair lift and float, tugged by the invisible current spilling from the smoke, the energy pushing outward in steady waves. The weight of it steadies me, roots me, even as adrenaline claws through my veins knowing the snake-like energy is awakened emboldens me.

I feel my eyes ignite with the same glowing shade of green that is swirling around my body, mirroring the coils licking against my skin. The magic whispers to me, low and insistent, stroking along the edges of my thoughts. It caresses my recklessness, breathes fire into the hunger in my chest, kisses the dark craving for destruction and chaos that is always waiting just beneath the surface of my skin.

"I thought I tasted you," Mezzel says while peering at me through the mask, "but you seemed so unsure. It was interesting to feel you watching me. It will be a pity if you die tonight with so much interest shown. I will be sure to summon you if you wish."

"Are you flirting with me?" I ask him with a delicate smile. "Are you going to fuck me like you fucked her?"

Mezzel does his little head tilt again, wondering how to answer such a question when hearing the blend of voices with mine. "Drink," he says, taking me slightly by surprise when offering me his chalice. "Drink and summon them. Call back all those you are here to save for yourself. Bring us their power so we may call our brothers and sisters from the grave, Necromancer. Your magic wants to play as much as your body wants to be played with."

"No thank you," my voice tells him. "I like to swallow directly from the man, not from his collection."

Mezzel is nothing but a ghost, draped in a used shell that does not belong to him. Every movement he is making is a lie, every breath he taking is borrowed. He walks on time that was granted but never reclaimed, a hollow thing animated by someone else's mistake and desires. Reclaiming lost souls is my curse. Summoning the dead is my torment. And he is both. He is everything I was born to fight and everything I cannot escape despite my best efforts to my whole life.

My fingers twitch, already trembling with the power straining to be set free. I don't have to think. I don't have to reach. The magic knows. It's carved into me. It's in my blood. In my bones. My soul. It was handed to me from my ancestors already singing a song of destruction.

All I need to do is let go. To loosen the leash. To let the part of me that existed before I even was explode and protect me like a lover enraged by the threat. Before this body, this moment, or this lifetime, this ancient inheritance, a burning legacy passed down through the line of women before me, has been waiting, always waiting, for the moment I would stop resisting and finally step aside. Somehow, I know this man before holds more of my past than just a this blurry memory. The way my magic is calling, the way my body is reacting, the way his eyes won't leave mine, I want him for my myself.

"Please don't make us do this," Mezzel asks calmly, soundly almost tired when he asks.

"Sorry," Jedrek replies. "You've triggered the witch. Now you're about to be spanked."

8

Now you're about to be spanked?" Mezzel repeats, his tone mocking. "Really, Jedrek? Your wit is slipping." Jedrek nods in defeat, slumping his shoulders in his tight black shirt looking almost bored. "It's been a long night. Can we just kill you and go home?"

Mezzel removes his deer skull mask with one golden clawed glove to reveal a heavily scared face. The scars are healed in jagged lines, but his brown eyes are alive with a fury I don't fully understand. "You can try," he tells Jedrek.

But I don't want to kill him. The magic whispers something darker, something more intimate. It coils through my ribs, urging me toward him. My breath rips ragged from my lungs, trembling with hunger. My body clenches with a desire I never thought I would have, but here it is, riding me harder than any man ever has before in my life.

"Or..." I tell him, my voice smoky with temptation, "you could belong to me instead of Hell." Green smoke slides from my fingers, winding around his body like a lover's touch.

Jedrek sighs again, letting the word, "Fuck," mingle with the air escaping his lungs.

Mezzel places the chalice down upon one of the ledges of the main hall with his mask while the smoke entwines around him. I watch as he randomly shivers under its embrace.

"Why would I do that?" Mezzel asks honestly, relaxing and letting my magic play with him.

"I can bring back all of those you have lost," my voice flirts with his true desires, coaxing him, dipping into his hunger.

"Harper," I hear Jedrek caution.

"And you would do this why?" Mezzel asks again, his voice fraying at the seams, the pleasure pressing him thin.

"I need an army. You need a sanctuary," the good-girl part of me answers first. The one who is always thinking of duty, but then the other part of me finally cuts in. "And I want you to fuck me. When I want you to fuck me. Exactly like how you fuck."

Mezzel had closed his eyes to further enjoy my magic slowly stroking him but now he is staring at me. "What will this cost me?"

"Your vessel," Jedrek answered for me with a bitterness I had not expected from him.

"I give you a wraith army to fuck and command and my vessel?" Mezzel muses, amused with the boldness of the request.

"I give you your family and a home. I give you respect, a true house to be respected, safety under my name. No. I don't want to fuck your whole house. Just you. I want you. All of you," I breathe the last words more than say them, wondering what my magic knows that I don't. Why is this dark part of me so attracted to him, craving him in a way that is taking over every part of me?

Mezzel walks to me, almost coming to stand directly in my face. He stares into my eyes, churning my soul, making me gasp with pleasure and just an edge of pain. "You want to be my Queen?" he whispers. "I can make you a Queen of the dead. Our rituals would bring your power to completion. You would be a true necromancer, a true Queen if you could trust me to protect you, worship you, keep you."

"Yes," I hear my voice whisper so gently back to him.

Mezzel leans in to close the remaining distance between the two of us, kissing my lips with just a brush of his across them, warming the flesh with his breath placing a promise between he and I for what is to come later. "I'll take you to my vessel."

Jedrek and I follow in silence. His stride is stiff, every movement taut. No jokes tumble from his mouth as we walk the long hallway behind the black robes. No sly glances my way. His eyes stay fixed forward, cold and unwavering with his blue gaze. That silence is worse than anything he could have said, and the knot in my stomach tells me I may have fucked up more than I realize.

My magic coils tight against my skin, wrapped so close it hovers just above me, an almost visible glow. The spirals twist and cling like smoke pressed into flesh, restless, waiting. It feels alive, tense, and hungry as though it's only biding its time until Mezzel steps too near, until it can rouse fully awake and taste him. Just as I, too, keep catching myself wondering what his lips might have tasted like.

The hall opens into a chamber, and the sight before me freezes me in place. My sanity thought it was safe after the previous showing of their rituals. It was wrong. I was wrong.

A woman is chained to the base of a towering stone angel, its hands clasped in a mock prayer, wings arching above her like a cruel parody of a sanctuary. A prayer was once carved into the base of the angel. Now, unreadable from blood and time, it further adds to the disparaging scene of torment. The rusted hinges from the iron gate surrounding the angel scream as Mezzel drags the gate open. The sound is a fitting dirge for the scene inside.

Her chains are thick, heavy enough to drag her to her knees. The weight of them etches exhaustion into her features, carving shadows under her eyes, pulling her body down. Still, she forces her head up, eyes fixed on us as we approach.

Her skin once perfect and untouched is marred with carved symbols, the same sigils etched into the white mask taken from the corpse of the last sacrifice Mezzel's silent companion now cradles in his hand. Lines slice across her flesh, marks pointing in every direction, cruel geometry-like scars twisting her body into a map.

She isn't just a prisoner. She's a spell, a living incantation bound to their will, her own flesh is the parchment they've written on. Her only modesty is the tangled fall of blonde hair draped across her bare body, too thin a curtain to hide what they've done to her.

"Shhhhhhh," Mezzel lovingly tells her, petting her face when he nears her. "I have what you need," he whispers kissing her forehead as he hands over the chalice to her.

Despite the weight of the chains dragging her down, she lifts her hands eagerly when he offers the chalice. Her fingers tremble against the iron links, but there's no hesitation. She drinks deep, greedily swallowing the contents as though the thick, metallic mixture is nectar instead of filth. No coaxing. No force. She wants it. Needs it. She's been waiting for him. Waiting for this, just as he said she would be.

The dark red liquid runs down the corner of her mouth, streaking across the carved symbols of her skin before she licks it away with devotion that makes my stomach turn. She almost purrs with the last swallow as if she can taste the sexual release which has brought her the concoction. Her face relaxes into a mask of sexual satisfaction, staring up at Mezzel with complete reverence for making it happen.

I stand back with Jedrek, watching this play out with a sick disbelief I can't put into words. My whole body screams *what the actual fuck* and for once my mouth doesn't.

I've seen vessels before. The empty shells drained of everything. They normally hate their keepers or are stripped of humanity entirely to ensure their obedience. That's what vessels are supposed to be.

But this? This is something else. Something in between kept and punished. Her eyes burn with hunger even as the chains bite into her wrists, as if she's both a prisoner and a disciple to them. Not fully hostage. Not fully free. She's a willing participant shackled in iron and bound by symbols carved in blood.

And that's worse. So much worse. Especially considering what we still have to do to her.

"Still want that wraith army?" Jedrek whispers to me. "Or Mezzel as a snuggle buddy?"

If I was sane, I'd tell him no, but that would also be admitting I might have made a mistake. I'm not going to do that. "Yes," I answer tasting bile. "Can't wait. So excited."

"Mmhhhmm," Jedrek tests. "I bet."

The blonde finishes the last of the offering with closed eyes and a soft sigh, her whole body sagging in the chains as though she has found completion. Fulfillment. She looks almost as serene as the angel above her. For a brief moment, I wonder if I, too, should be saying a prayer for her.

Mezzel takes the chalice from her limp hand. His clawed fingers brush his knuckles across her face before he begins to pet her hair. Each slow stroke pulls her deeper into that false calm, lulling her into relaxation. There is a tenderness to it, wrong and obscene, but tender all the same. Something that feels like a bond, more than vessel and master. Something which somehow shouldn't exist, but here it is, right in front of me.

His gloved hand slides again through her tangled hair, and she leans into it each time, chasing the contact searching for her comfort. She does not see him draw the curved blade from behind the stone angel. She does not notice how he is leaning to keep something from her view.

I see his face clearly now with the deer mask discarded at the angel's base. Not just the flash he gave us to unsettle us with his threat or the adjustment he made to seal our bargain, but the full view of the man he has been placed into by a necromancer long ago. His scars catch the light, the twisted lines of old wounds shifting with every flicker of emotion he does not bother to hide. It twists something inside of me. Maybe pity? Maybe sorrow as I watch him?

His gaze stays on her, his head tilted with the same unnatural focus he has had all night. But now, just for a heartbeat, his expression wavers. Sadness. It's sadness. All the Gods help me. It's sadness.

And then he turns that potent look on us.

My chest tightens as he grips her chin, forcing her head high with a lover's touch. She does not fight him. She does not even open her eyes. She tilts willingly into his hold, blind to the blade arcing around behind her neck.

The steel kisses her skin in silence. One smooth pull. A line of red opening against pale flesh as we watch.

She never saw it coming. Never gasped. Never cried out. She simply folded, sliding to the floor like a marionette with its strings cut. Even in death, her features remained soft, as if she slipped away dreaming. Like the stone angel she was chained to, she wept without a sound as her blood spilled, staining the altar at her knees.

Then the air split.

The many soul fragments she carried inside her ripped free, swirling past me soundlessly in a rush of heat and light. They tore toward the unseen, desperate to return to the places where they once belonged, racing to become whole. Jedrek and I did nothing to collect them. We did not need to. Their escape meant they would fly to Lucifer's keeping, whole again, collected like lost treasures. With any luck, that would be enough to satisfy him tonight and it would spare us another visit from him or his little friends. At the very least, now, I can shower.

"My part is complete," Mezzel tells me, ignoring the demon beside me who made the price nonnegotiable. "Now, when do we begin, my Queen?"

My stomach turns to raw emotions of twists and turns as he stares at me. "Soon as we clean up all of your mistakes," I tell him with my stomach praying it buys me some time.

I don't understand this yearning I have for him. I want to caress every scar upon his face. Hear every one of his stories which put them there. He tastes of old magic, a sharp whiskey with a fire which would warm the deepest depression.

Something just dark enough that would dare to die for you, or kill for you, and I want to dine on this flavor every night.

"Mortals don't like the whole dead body dumping," Jedrek points to the woman. "Something about it being rude to the deceased."

I turn my head to look at Jedrek with a stare of lack of comprehension for his sudden rudeness. "And a little hard to explain."

Jedrek tosses his head slightly back-and-forth weighing out my answer before rolling his eyes and nodding. "Yeah. I guess that's true, too. Wouldn't want the locals to think some weird sex magic is happening in the local cemetery. Wait.....," he let's his sentence trail off point at Mezzel and the mute one with mock shock. "Whatever will we tell the local PTA?" He covers his mouth after asking with false fear. "They are going to ban the cemetery now."

Mezzel is not amused by Jedrek. He gives a short tilt of his head, and the other man moves to unchain the blonde. The process is loud, the heavy rattle of links clattering against stone as the weight falls around her feet and the base of the angel statue.

Once she is freed, Mezzel runs his gloved hand slowly through her hair, combing it back with deliberate care. Slowly, he removes his gloves with a deep sigh. His bare hands trail the length of her body, touching her as though he is claiming each piece, before pressing them flat against her pale flesh.

His eyes find mine as it begins.

Her body collapses in on itself, wilting and withering like a flower left in a drought. Her skin puckers, tightening, her flesh sinking against bone that turns brittle and flakes away. The chains once holding her fall heavy to the floor as her body peels back into nothing. Her blood seeps and then dries into dust, lifting off the floor as if carried by a breeze. a breeze that I cannot feel and should not exist inside a closed chamber.

In the space of a breath, she is gone. Flesh, bone, and blood reduced to dust and ash, scattered, and carried away as though she had never been here at all. Yet, the sadness of it, that she has left like an echo which shall forever haunt this space. Her name may never have a golden plaque, but the angel will always be sleeping here just the same.

"Her family will never know what's happened to her," I tell him with sadness.

"She had no family, my Queen. If she did, they have long passed. She was over one hundred years," Mezzel says, straightening his black robe as he stands.

"She looked to be maybe in her twenties," I argue suddenly very self-conscious.

Mezzel nods. "That's when she became my vessel. I shall clean the other and then find you." He turns to stare directly at me. "I will always find you, my Queen. You are mine. I now possess you."

Something clicked mentally for me when he said those words. He doesn't just want to possess my body. He wants to reach the depths of my desires until he possesses my soul, branding me forever as his. I will be possessed forever and it's not by the man I thought would be holding me.

"A wraith army?" Jedrek is pacing my living room floor like a caged animal while I sip on one of the few gifts God has ever given me. Coffee. "Do you have any idea what you have done?"

"Nothing yet," I chuckle from pure exhaustion, "Other than avoid having to fight someone you didn't seem to keen on fighting. You could just say, *wow Harper thanks for thinking of a way that didn't cause me to get my ass kicked."*

Jedrek shakes his head slowly causing his dark hair to fall over his face. "Harper, I would have rather gotten my ass kicked for the both of us than for you to have to deal with the risks of a wraith army. Much less had you deal with a wraith fuck boy you've made out of that scarred freak, Mezzel."

"Okay, you know I received the same lecture from many about you?" I smile over my mug at him letting the steam kiss my lips as I wait his reaction.

He stops his pacing to stare at me with a smile widening across his face. "I'm sure you did. Wait till those same ones giving that lecture find out about this. I might just have to be here for it. It's not often I'm the lesser evil in someone's life."

"Can't picture you the lesser evil," I lift an eyebrow, sipping the only thing which might allow me the energy to finish this lecture.

"You're about to," he exhales as he collapses in the recliner across the room from me. "Why? Can you just help me understand why?"

"The magic wanted him," I answer as best as I can while trying to hide behind the black mug with pink sparkles. "I tend to let it do it's thing since everyone love to keep reminding me, I'm so new to all of this. It seems to know better than I do what to do in situations, anyway."

Jedrek drops his head into his hands. "The magic wanted him," he repeats with each word laced with disbelief. "Your half-feral, starved-for-chaos magic?"

"Um," I stall, "Yeah. That magic."

"Your borderline dark magic?" he presses. "Your near to almost sex-magic itself?"

I don't answer. I just stare at him from over the rim of the mug as I sip the life saving dark brew. Does he really need an answer?

"Of course it wanted him," he reclines back into the chair. "Wraiths are wild magic. They are death from a wish list, something that someone dreamed up and stitched together into a body. Now he wants you to do the same over and over again. Are you even ready for such a task?"

I hope so, I think to myself. To him I answer, "Sure. How different could it be from what I do every night?"

Jedrek lifts one eyebrow hearing my answer. "We are so fucked."

"You were the one who said you liked to see what trouble I can drag us into," I reminded him.

"I meant your witchy shit," he throws his hands up. "Not summoning old souls with a vengeance list and a sex drive to make teenagers envious."

"I've upgraded," I offer with a shrug and dangerous smirk.

"Downgraded, Harper. Downgraded," Jedrek says letting all the air out of his whole body.

"You still haven't said exactly what the risk is," I remind him. "He didn't seem that horrible."

Jedrek sits up, his palms pressing flat to the wooden table between us. His voice is steady, but there is an edge to it. "Wraiths are loyal to a degree that is terrifying, Harper. Which is great if Mezzel is serious about you being their Queen. But if he isn't, they will tear you apart without warning. The same thing happens if they even think their Queen has betrayed them. They are hive-minded, and it looks like Mezzel will be their leader. You keep him happy, you won't have a problem. The second, the very second, he decides you are up to something, there will not be a conversation. You will be dead. Anyone who stands with you will be dead. No amount of warm memories, or nights spent together will sway him."

His eyes harden as he continues. "The more of them there are, the quicker your death will be. They are strong, fast, and nearly impossible to kill. They are already dead. The only way to end them is complete beheading. And that loyalty works both ways. The slightest insult, the smallest betrayal he perceives towards you, that person is gone. No discussion. No second chances. You are going to have to explain to him, over and over, how you live your life with that sarcasm of yours.

Otherwise, he will try to kill everyone around you, and he will succeed. It will become his whole focus to succeed."

He leans closer, voice dropping low. "They are the ideal nightmare. And you just adopted an army of them. You invited them to become a house of their own without a single word to the other houses."

I hold his gaze, my eyes even with his. "You mean the other houses who are constantly trying to kill me? Those houses?" I ask without flinching under his warnings. "So, you are telling me the vampires just lost their crown as most terrifying? You want to send them the memo, or shall I?"

Jedrek does not blink. "I am telling you if you truly are their Queen, you are the most terrifying. Even above and below will have to rethink their positions when visiting now."

The silence that follows says more than his words. Above and below do not rethink. They erase. Natural disasters tend to take care of any of their worries which keep them from visiting. It's why certain places keep having them.

"The Coven isn't coming back without some kind of buffer," I challenge him. "You're the keeper of the witches and yet the vampires are still holding a huge control, keeping us all in fear of what they may be doing next. I don't see them consulting any houses? I don't see them having this conversation with you? If I can't turn to you to control the vampires, and make the Coven feel safe, I warned you. I'll do what I have to do. Perhaps my magic is even done waiting for you to step up and do something?"

His fingers begin to drum along the wood's edge after hearing my words. "There is only so much I can do for my witches. Free will is a bitch, remember?"

"Vampires are still alive, unpunished and yet Lucifer trusts you so much he allows you to suck on his cock? Normally when you are sucking the bosses dick it's to get something you want like a raise, a higher job position, or I don't know, someone in trouble," I mock. "And here you were mocking that poor woman that she was doing it wrong while you just sit with a mouthful of cum and nothing to show for it."

"Careful, Harper," he tells me with a lowered voice. "I knew some of those witches longer than you have been alive."

"And yet you let them die or be forced from their home?" I ask wondering why my death wish is so strong. "Do you still smell their blood soaked into the carpets and walls or have you just moved past all of that in search for the next fuck during your dry months?"

I saw him move but I didn't register how fast he moved until he was on top of me.

"Shut your fucking mouth," he whispers into my face, leaning over me, his blue eyes raging. "That bitch is getting everything she deserves in the other realm."

"While the ones who did it are free out here," I hiss back into his face.

"I'm aware," he suffers each word on his tongue, but it's the watery glaze over his eyes which take my breath. "I have begged to have their hearts in my hands, but time and time again I have been refused. They have protection I have yet to discover, but when I do, I will kill those protecting them, too, Harper. I will kill them all."

My will to hurt him dissolves as the single tear rolls down his peach toned skin. One tear is all I need to be shown. Just a small token of emotion to let me know there is something in that heart of his for the witches we have lost and those who have yet to be found.

The apology never formed that I was preparing to give him. Instead, he was suddenly airborne, pushed across the room away from me and landing on all fours with a look of total expectation and entertainment as he stood.

"Are you alright?" Mezzel's voice comes from behind me turning my head with shock.

"Complete loyalty," Jedrek teases. "If he only has one Queen, that is."

I stand, sensing the stench of alpha male pheromones trying to compete in a small space. "Should I be worried?"

"About?" Mezzel asks, his eyes turning to a dark brown as they switch from Jedrek to me to return to Jedrek.

"You," I answer simply.

Mezzel rises from where he has been waiting for Jedrek. "No," he says, his voice steady as he extends one of those golden clawed gloved hands towards me. "I am yours to command and have, and you are mine to protect and take."

Something in his words hits me like a crack in a wall, loosening the bricks I have kept so carefully stacked around myself. His brown eyes draw me towards that hand, towards the promise waiting with his open palm. A promise that no one has ever offered me before. A promise, just once, the little girl inside me has always wanted to hear.

I am tired. Bone deep, soul deep, and still, I can see the strength he offers even through the shapeless robe. His broad shoulders. Those arms built to shield me. The idea of hiding behind them tempts me in a way I cannot mentally push away. I want his promise. I hate myself for wanting it. But I do.

When I take his hand, his grip is gentle, almost reverent. Slowly, carefully, he draws me forward, pulling me until my head rests against his chest. The sound of his heart beating steady in my ear brings me instant calm, raising questions I am not ready to ask. I fall into him, somewhat ashamed to be doing so in front of Jedrek, but my soul feels to be stretching through my skin to join with this man.

One arm encircles me, firm enough to hold me but light enough to soothe away the doubts. The other strokes along my back in slow, calming arcs. My body responds before my mind can resist, answering to something in him that feels older than this life. As though I have felt this energy before, carried it inside me once.

All I know in this moment is how right it feels. And how dangerous it is that it feels amazing to every part of me.

"You have nothing to fear from me, my Queen," Mezzel whispers into my ear. "It's you who could destroy me with just a thought, my dark necromancer, and yet still, I'm daring the risk to fall for you."

"That redhead is taken," I hear Jedrek warn. "You're her guard, wraith. Nothing more."

Mezzel's hand never slowed, or strayed, from his soothing motion and touch upon my back, but he still dared Jedrek by saying, "We'll see, demon."

"Fun fact," I insert, pushing myself away from them both to head down to my bedroom, "it seems my coffee is cold. That's gross and depressing. Which means I'm headed to bed. Good night to you both. Enjoy the dick measuring."

Mezzel begins to follow me, but Jedrek is quick to stop him. "And you are going where, Mezzel?"

I watch from the top of the stairs as Mezzel removes Jedrek's hand from his chest. "I'm her guard, as you stated. Where do you think I am going? You are a demon, where do you think you are going?"

I shouldn't be enjoying this. The feminism part of me should be eye rolling and gagging, but she's on mute. The fan girl part of me is wanting snacks and baby oil. I'm not totally ashamed.

"She's a witch. I'm in charge of her, as Lucifer has ordered," Jedrek counters. "I guess I'm sitting right here on the couch all night to be sure you understand that."

Mezzel, with his normal calm tone, looks at Jedrek to say, "If you wish," before pulling the deer mask from his robe to place it over his face. "You can listen to her scream my name all night should you decide. It won't bother me that you are up here."

I am suddenly speechless, wet, and throbbing. I don't know if it's from him shutting Jedrek up, the sight of the mask with its brown eyes closing in on me, or both, but it doesn't matter. My thighs are slick again, my body aching for him. My eyes are locked on Mezzel and his are locked on me. By the time he reaches me, turning me, pressing me down the stairs, I can already feel the thick, brutal hardness under his robe shoving against me, demanding I acknowledge it. The gasp escaping my mouth is all the approval he needs.

"How shall I take you?" His voice is a growl, his gloved hands tearing at my clothes before I can even answer.

"I want to see you while you fuck me," I pant, already undone just from the scrape of leather across my bare skin.

"So, you shall."

He doesn't waste another word. He throws me against the wall at the bottom of the stairs and slams himself into me.

The pain tears a cry from my throat, sharp and broken, my body screaming at the same impossible stretch the other woman was fighting to endure. For a moment I can't breathe. I can't think from it. I remember the mausoleum. I remember the way he split her open and how she barely took him in her mouth. And here I am, split on him, legs locked around his waist as if I stand a chance of surviving the very thing which has been dancing with my dark desires all night. My nails claw at him, my body ready to unravel, but he catches my eyes through the mask and pins me there.

"Relax," he softly coaxes. "Give me your trust."

Something inside me shatters and melts all at once. My body yields.

"Trust," he softly pleads again, dragging me down onto him with his hands on my ass until I choke on the scream tearing out of me.

He fucks me open with punishing patience, each deliberate push working me wider, deeper, until I'm clinging to him, nails biting through his robe and into his flesh. His eyes never leave mine, a predator watching its prey submit. I try to close mine, but every time I do the sheer violence of the stretch rips them open again, and he's there, staring back at me, keeping me grounded in this moment through the pain.

When he finally seats himself all the way inside, my scream breaks into a sob of surrender. My body explodes, soaking him, coming hard just from being filled. He moans behind the mask, and then he moves, pounding me against the wall, finally able to freely move inside of me. The wet slap of our bodies is almost obscene and echoing through my basement room. His moans rip out in ragged bursts, raw and feral, until they twist into words.

"Say my name. Say it while I fuck you."

I can barely think, can barely breathe, but he doesn't stop. His hips slam harder, deeper, making me scream with each thrust while he almost abuses my body with unspent emotions from tonight.

"Say it!" he commands, slamming into me until the air leaves my lungs.

"Mezzel!" I cry, and the sound only fuels him.

"Mezzel!" I scream again, broken, desperate, begging for more. I want to be destroyed, releasing my own locked grief and guilt. "Please, Mezzel, harder!"

"Yes," he shouts as an answer to my screaming, his rhythm savage, unrelenting, driving me up the wall like I weigh nothing.

My body is his to use, his to ruin, and I give him everything. My voice is nothing but screams, sobs, his name over and over until it sounds like prayer, pleading for a salvation only he can grant me.

And then I see Jedrek. Sitting on my bed. Watching. Watching not only us, but my face, locked onto my eyes as I stare into Mezzel's. The shame slams into my chest like a blade.

"Ignore him," Mezzel whispers seeing my guilt, his hand on my jaw forcing my face back to his. "Stay with me. Look at me. Just me."

His eyes devour me, ripping the shame apart and turning it into more heat, more need. The edge is softened. The pace may be the same, but the urge has a different message now.

"Stay with me, my Queen," he whispers, slowing just enough to make me ache before he surges back into me. "You are beautiful. Trust me. Let me worship you."

I can't fight it. My head tips back, my body surrendering again. He pounds into me mercilessly, wet, savage thrusts that leave me crying his name like if I were to stop saying it he might disappear. My thighs burn, my lungs burn, my nails rake his flesh, but I don't stop. I'm too scared to stop.

"Do it," he commands, his voice low and dangerous. "Come for me. I have you. I'm right here."

My whole body locks and breaks, release ripping through me like a wildfire, devouring everything in its path. He pins me to the wall, almost pounding me through it as his own climax tears out of him. Heat floods inside me, thick and hot, spilling deep until I can feel nothing else.

"My Queen," he chants, over and over, his voice muffled against my neck, guttural and wild. "My Queen. My Queen."

I can't see. My vision is white. My legs are gone. My body is ruined. And I don't care.

Every ounce of me is shattered and claimed by him. It was worth it. I am possessed and I still haven't had a shower.

"Enjoyed yourself?" Mezzel finally questions Jedrek from the curve of my neck.

"I hope you share, wraith," Jedrek tells him as he stands to leave, "because I don't plan to simply give up on her."

"I would think less of you if you did," Mezzel tells him with a mocking tone, "but no, I don't."

"Then I guess you and I are going to have a problem," Jedrek warns him before he fades into the shadows to return to wherever he goes when he leaves me.

Mezzel lowers me from where he has been holding me, helping me back to the floor. His brown eyes are tender, so very gentle, filled with concern as he does this. "Are you hurt?"

"If I am, I'll never complain," I try to smile, cringing inside hearing my attempt at flirting.

Mezzel tilts his head, removing the deer mask to fully see me. "You're worried about something."

"I am," I nod hating the after sex small talk. "Look, I'm flattered about this whole alpha male bullshit territory pissing match you two have going on, but I'm not the girl that's worth it. I'm a mess. In so many ways. Ways that aren't fun. At least not always fun, anyway."

"Get in bed," he softly commands, making me wonder about this whole queen title.

But I obey, making me also wonder about this whole queen title.

Mezzel pulls together my blankets into something that resembles a bedding set, never once judging me, at least out loud, for the state of my bed.

"May I join you?" he softly asks with his body tensing, prepared to be told 'no' by me.

I answer him by pulling the same blankets back he had just spread around me.

I watch with a lifted eyebrow as he pulls the weapons from his glove, his belted area, his boots as he removes them and the back of his robe knowing he was just fucking me rather rapidly with all of those sharp objects rattling around. He places his mask, and the weapons, on a chair he pulls to serve as nightstand beside his side of the bed. I don't ask why the mask has to face us. At least not tonight. Tonight, I won't even notice it in a few moments when my body gives up on today. In the morning, when I roll over, it will scare the shit out of me.

Laying on his back, he lifts his arm to offer me his chest to sleep on without me having to ask or us having to exchange words. He already knows my frigid ego. I want to pretend I don't want the offer. Except, I waste no time snuggling up to him, drowning in the many scents of his robe and the skin underneath it. Relaxing under the weight of his arm as he holds me, I realize I'm sleeping with a man I just met, literally.

"I used to mock women like me," I whisper to the folds of his robe.

"Hmmm?" he asks with a soft sound of curiosity.

"I don't know you and here I am having sex with you and now you are in my bed," I hear my voice crack with my rambling.

"You know me," he whispers. "You just don't remember."

"I think I would remember a man in a deer mask," I meant it as a joke, but it comes out a soft crying sound with my shame.

His hand strolls down the flesh of my back to soothe me. "We didn't wear deer masks when your mother was the vessel. That didn't start until the new mistress came into power."

"I swear to fuck if you confess you used to sleep with my mother," I warn him.

Mezzel laughs hearing me. "No, Harper. I was just a soldier then. Not a Queen's guard. I wasn't worthy of your mother, but we met. You were a little girl then. Curious. Vibrant. When they came for the vessel, your mother, I should have taken you with us. You belonged with us, but we left you with the witches, thinking they would protect you. They failed you, and in that regard, we failed you. I failed you, Harper. I swear to you. I won't fail you, again."

"Why didn't you say anything in the mausoleum?" I pull away but he holds me too tight to do so.

"Would you have believed me then?" Mezzel asks. "It was so hard to finally be standing across from you. Something I never thought would be possible in your lifetime. Only to see the disgust in your eyes at our ritual, with me, with who I've become. When your magic finally 'saw' me, I wanted to cry. You were to be mine by our rights. Now, after all these years of them keeping us apart, you are to finally be mine."

"Keeping us apart?"

Mezzel sighs, just as mentally exhausted as I am, but I keep pushing. "Please, my Queen, let us sleep. This body needs to rest even if I do not. I will answer everything, tell you everything, *be* your everything, but for now, you will sleep in my arms, and I will keep you safer than you have ever been. I'm here now, Harper. I'm so sorry it took me so long to reach you, but I'm here now. You're safe. You're finally safe."

I don't push him. I let him reach up beside my bed and flip the light switch that will cast my room into complete darkness, something which normally terrifies me. Each night until now I have had to sleep with the bathroom light on. Allowing just enough light to at least chase the gloom from the corners of my room if it can't chase it from the corners of my mind. Just enough light to convince me the monsters are far enough away from my bed to allow me to sleep, but I swear I am the leader of the house of witches.

Tonight, my heart doesn't drop as the darkness sweeps across the room. A heavy arm rests across my body holding me secure against my fears, protecting me from any of the monsters which may slip into the darkness unnoticed by me. The other arms rests on his chest allowing his hand to hold my own, rubbing his thumb across it to settle any nerves fraying under today's lingering events. He kisses the top of my head before sinking his own back into his pillow forming his wordless, gentle 'good night' leaving me wondering if this is now the rest of my life and what GiGi would think if she were still here.

"Mezzel," I whisper into the darkness.

"Hmmm," his voice vibrates underneath me.

"Please don't kill Regan if she comes home?" I ask him.

"Who is Regan?" he asks half asleep, half awake, half interested.

"Please, my guard, let us sleep. This body needs rest even if you do not. I will answer everything, tell you everything, *be* your everything, but for now, I will sleep in your arms and feel safe as I have never felt safe before because you are here now. You are finally here, Mezzel. As long as it took for you to reach me, you are finally here. I'm safe. I'm finally safe."

Mezzel says nothing as I repeat his words back to him. I feel him stiffen underneath me, but he says nothing.

"Because you are mine to command and have and I am yours to protect and take," I whisper, hearing his ragged breath when I say the final words.

Mezzel lowers his head to the top of my head, saying into my hair, "I'm going to fall in love with you, aren't I?"

"I think I already am," I sink further into his robe, trying to hide from the world and my own truth.

Sometimes the world allows us to build swords and shields from our wit and walls. Sometimes it allows us to build them from our hearts. Sometimes, just sometimes, it lets us build them from behind those who love us. That's when you know life is waiting to fuck you.

Extras

Want to know follow Mezzel and Harper's story further? Make sure you're caught up on The Great Hexpextations Series to discover more about Mezzel in the upcoming new release, *The Hidden Secrets*.

About the Author

Marie F Crow weaves her stories around the human element of the horror verses the 'monsters' themselves. She believes that the real horror of life does not come from the expected, but from the unexpected responses of the human nature and what depths of trauma a person must survive in certain situations. She began writing The Risen Series when feeling that the popular genre was slipping too deep into the realm of pure 'slasher' and forgetting what the horror of zombies can mean for a story.

Now, with her children's series launched, Marie hopes to use her favorite 'monster' as a teaching tool to inspire children to understand that not everything that looks scary, is scary.

With Abigail and Her Pet Zombie series, Marie hopes to further spread her love for all things "that go bump in the night" with small children showing them that it's okay to be different and to embrace those same differences in those around them.

Facebook: @MarieFCrow.Author
Instagram: @authormariefcrow
Twitter: @MarieFCrow

Please consider leaving a review. Any and all feedback is appreciated. Even if you just leave a star rating. Every bit helps other readers find the book.

Also by the Author

The Risen Series

Dawning
Margaret
Remnants
Courage
Defiance

A Risen Series Novel

Genny

The Siren Series

Crown of Betrayal
Crown of Remorse
Crown of Conquest

The Great Hexpectation Series

The Little Lies
The Broken Hearted
The Whispered Words
The Hidden Secrets (Coming Soon)

The Great Hexpectation Novella

Possessed
Enthralled (Coming Soon)
Reaped (Coming Soon)

The Abigail and her Pet Zombie Series

Illustrated Children's Books

Abigail and her Pet Zombie
Zoo Day

Spring
Summer
Halloween
Happy Birthday
A Very Zombie Christmas

The Abigail and her Pet Zombie Series
Beginner Chapter Books
Abigail and her Pet Zombie

Standalone Novels
The Witch I Am!

About the Publisher

Kingston Publishing Company, founded by C. K. Green, is dedicated to providing authors an affordable way to turn their dream into a reality. We publish over 100+ titles annually in multiple formats including print and ebook across all major platforms.

We offer every service you will ever need to take an idea and publish a story. We are here to help authors make it in the industry. We want to provide a positive experience that will keep you coming back to us. Whether you want a traditional publisher who offers all the amenities a publishing company should or an author who prefers to self-publish, but needs additional help - we are here for you.

Now Accepting Manuscripts!
Please send query letter and manuscript to:
submissions@kingstonpublishing.com

Visit our website at
www.kingstonpublishing.com

www.ingramcontent.com/pod-product-compliance
Lightning Source LLC
Chambersburg PA
CBHW071132100726
47908CB00008B/2583

* 9 7 8 1 6 4 5 3 3 5 4 0 5 *